SHIP *of* DOLLS

SHIP
of
DOLLS

SHIRLEY PARENTEAU

CANDLEWICK PRESS

Copyright © 2014 by Shirley Parenteau

First edition 2014

Library of Congress Catalog Card Number 2014931695
ISBN 978-0-7636-7003-0

14 15 16 17 18 19 BVG 10 9 8 7 6 5 4 3 2 1

Printed in Berryville, VA, U.S.A.

This book was typeset in Walbaum.

Candlewick Press
99 Dover Street
Somerville, Massachusetts 02144

visit us at www.candlewick.com

For Gail, my sister and best friend.
And with a special thank-you
to my beautiful daughter-in-law,
Miwa Takamura Parenteau,
for telling me of Hinamatsuri.

CHAPTER 1

Portland, Oregon
Late November, 1926

I dare you. I double-dare you." Beneath the tweed cap that matched his belted coat, Jack Harmon's brown eyes glowed. Grandma said he had the makings of a good-looking man. Eleven-year-old Lexie Lewis couldn't see it. Jack was a neighbor and a classmate, but she didn't trust him.

"Go in and hold that doll—the one that's going to the girls' festival in Japan." Jack motioned toward the school's front door and the hall that led to the sixth-grade room. "Then come back and, to prove you did it, tell me if the doll's dress has buttons in the back."

Lexie hesitated, watching others from school splashing through the rain on their way home. A motorcar rumbled past, making them jump back from flying water. Grandpa said this winter wasn't as wet as winters were when he was a boy, but it was wet enough for Lexie. It rained even more here in Portland than it did in Seattle. Maybe it seemed that way because she didn't belong here. She belonged in Seattle with Mama.

"Miss Tompkins won't let anyone touch her," she said finally. As if Jack didn't already know that.

"So what's she gonna do if she catches you? Cut off your hand?" He leaned against the school's front-porch rail. "You helped bake cakes and stuff to buy the doll. Why shouldn't you pick her up?"

The class was still collecting pennies to send the doll to Japan for a girls' festival called Hinamatsuri. Classes and clubs all over America were preparing dolls, thousands of them. Lexie's class had voted to name their doll Emily Grace, but none of the students were allowed to touch her.

Lexie shook her head. "Miss Tompkins doesn't want dirty fingers smudging the doll and her fancy dress."

"Are your hands dirty?"

"No!"

"So you're just scared."

"I am not!"

"Then here's your chance. Miss Tompkins left. Go in and pick up the doll. I dare you!"

Mama would have never refused a dare. But Lexie wasn't living with Mama now. She lived with her grandparents, and this was the kind of impulse Grandma was determined to root out of her.

Reason enough to do it, Lexie decided. She pulled open the door and walked quickly down the hall, but she wasn't just taking Jack's dare. Miss Tompkins wasn't being fair. And neither was Grandma.

The last students hurried past on their way out of the building. She hoped Jack was right, that Miss Tompkins had gone, too, back to the room she rented in the boardinghouse Jack's mother ran. Carefully, Lexie cracked open the door to the sixth-grade classroom, with its green paper wreath decorated with red glass balls.

The motion of the door made the balls clink together. She drew a sharp breath. What if someone heard? For a long moment, she stood still, every muscle tight, while she listened. The only sound was rain dripping from the eaves outside.

She peeked into the room, smelling chalk dust. Someone had slapped blackboard erasers together to clean them. And not long ago.

Again, she worried. *If Miss Tompkins is still here, what can I say to explain coming back?* She couldn't think of anything that wouldn't be a lie. And she couldn't say Jack had dared her to touch the doll. That would get them both in trouble.

She pushed the door open wider, an inch at a time, until she could see the entire room. Her breath whooshed out in a sigh of relief. No one was there. She hurried past the still-warm woodstove to the teacher's desk at the front.

The wooden box holding Emily Grace with her wicker suitcase was no longer on top of Miss Tompkins's desk. Lexie went around the desk to look at the closed drawers, picturing the box in her mind. Would it fit in a drawer? Or was it too big?

After an uneasy glance toward the hall, she tried the large bottom drawer. It slid out but held only notebooks. She closed it quickly, then remembered the storage closet at the back of the room.

She darted over. The round glass knob turned in her hand. The door squeaked open. After another glance toward the hall, she slipped inside and reached up to pull the chain to the lightbulb.

No one was going to cut off her hand, but if she was caught, she could expect a good scolding. Miss Tompkins never used the paddle the way some teachers did, but Grandma might hear about it. Grandma had strong ideas about proper behavior.

Where was Emily Grace? Boxes and stacks of books and papers crowded the shelves, along with a few old slates for writing. The box with the doll was not among them.

"She took Emily Grace home so nobody would touch her!" The words burst from Lexie. She could almost see Miss Tompkins leaving the school with the box under one arm. "And Jack must have known that. The skunk!"

His dare was one more way to get rid of her. Jack would do almost anything to avoid walking from school with her and getting teased by his friends. In the three months since she'd moved here from Seattle to live with her grandparents, Jack's mother and Grandma Lewis had insisted they walk together. They seemed to think one of those fast-moving motorcars would run right over her without Jack along.

As if she'd run in front of an automobile after what had happened to Papa.

Lexie took a deep breath, turned out the light

in the storeroom, and walked toward the front porch. As she neared the open door, a girl's voice said clearly, "Don't tell Lexie Lewis."

Lexie moved nearer. Louise Wilkins stood on the porch with her friend Alma Miller, whose father worked in Mr. Wilkins's department store.

"You know how she is," Louise added, "always trying to be the best. Anyway, it's a secret. Nobody's supposed to know yet."

"You'll win that trip to San Francisco, Louise," Alma said, as if her father's job depended on her agreeing with his boss's daughter. "I just know you'll write the best letter, the one chosen to go to Japan with Emily Grace."

"But don't tell Lexie," Louise warned again.

Letters? All the girls in the class were writing letters, hoping theirs would be chosen to go with the doll. None of the boys were interested in a festival just for girls, even one far away in Japan. When Miss Tompkins had asked if any of the boys would like to write a letter, Ollie Johnson had made a joke of the kind they might write: "'She'll be a good citizen. She won't spit or make rude noises at the table.'" All the boys laughed and began making noises. Miss Tompkins rang her handbell loudly for silence and didn't invite them again.

Nothing had been said about a trip to San Francisco, though. Lexie knew she wasn't likely to learn anything from Louise and Alma. Those two had made moving to Portland, Oregon — away from Mama — even harder than it had to be. Still, she had to ask. Lexie stalked onto the porch. "Don't tell me what?"

Both girls looked up. Louise tossed back her perfectly bobbed hair. "You don't need to know, Dog Breath."

Dog Breath. She was never going to live down eating a cookie after Jack had let a dog lick it. When she'd learned the truth and rinsed her mouth again and again in the fountain, Jack had walked home without her. Jack Harmon had a lot to answer for.

"Why would you care what we're talking about?" Alma asked. "You're not going to San Francisco. Your own mother doesn't want you — ouch!"

Louise must have pinched her for mentioning San Francisco. Lexie wanted to pinch her again for her nasty comment about Mama, but decided Alma wasn't worth the trouble. Could it be true? Could the girl who wrote the best letter be going with the doll to the send-off party in San Francisco? Well, so what if it was true? She didn't want to go south to San Francisco. That was the wrong direction. She wanted to go north, back to Seattle and Mama.

"You're right," Lexie told Alma. "I don't care." She walked past, swishing her skirt the way Mama did when ladies raised their noses while she passed, making sure they saw her not caring.

"It's just a rumor, anyway," Louise called. "Nobody knows if it's true."

"Like everything else you say," Lexie shot back as she headed toward her grandparents' house.

She didn't care that someone might go to San Francisco when thousands of dolls left for Japan to make friends with children there, but she did care about everything else.

She shouldn't be here living with strict grandparents. She cared about that a lot. She should be with Mama, happy and laughing and being *"the two of us together, kiddo."*

Mama liked to say she was a true modern flapper, that she and her friends had fun without worrying much about rules. That was almost funny, since Mama had sent Lexie to grandparents who believed that following rules was the only way to live.

But Mama said two years was long enough to be a widow. Lexie could almost see her snapping her fingers, her eyes sparkling while her love for life shimmered like sunbeams around her. The next thing Lexie knew, Mama married Toby, who played saxophone in the jazz club where she sang. And Toby said a little girl shouldn't live with parents who worked all night and slept all day.

"So here I am," Lexie said aloud. She slapped one hand against the flat-topped gatepost at the end of her grandparents' walk, then paused to add with a rush of defiance, "But I won't stay."

She took care to scrape her shoes on the mat before opening the back door. Grandma didn't like dirt tracked over her clean linoleum floor. When Lexie stepped inside, Grandma looked up from the kitchen stove and wiped her hands on the big apron she wore over her dress.

Grandma refused to bob her hair, even though Grandpa teased her about not keeping up with the times. She wouldn't cut the neat braids wrapped around her head even to wear the stylish cloche hat Mama had given her. Sometimes Lexie suspected that Grandma kept her old-fashioned style *because* of Mama.

"There you are, Electra," Grandma said. "I've been watching for you." She pulled an envelope from a deep pocket in her apron. "That flapper finally remembered she has a daughter and took time from her busy life to write to you."

CHAPTER 2

"From Mama? There's a letter from Mama?" Maybe Toby had changed his mind. Maybe she could be with Mama again. Could she go tonight? Hope pounded through Lexie. "What did Mama say?"

Grandma placed the letter on the kitchen table beside a glass of milk and an oatmeal cookie on a plate. "I do not open other people's mail."

Lexie believed that her grandma loved her. She just didn't want her to grow up to be a flapper like Mama. And she couldn't forget that Papa—her only son—had died driving the fast motorcar Mama had begged him to buy.

Lexie couldn't forget, either. She knew that Papa had wanted the car as much as Mama had. But sometimes Lexie wished she and her mother had both been with him when he took it for a spin that night. Then they would all be together now in heaven.

But this was no time for dark thoughts. The envelope was like an extra Christmas present, one she wouldn't save for Christmas. She made herself swallow some milk and take a bite of cookie, though, holding off the one thing she wanted most.

When she couldn't wait a second longer, she pried open the flap. Mama's spicy perfume wafted out, bringing an image so sharp, it was almost as if Mama stood laughing in front of her, stockings rolled below her knees, brown hair swinging against her ears in the shingled bob she loved, bright hazel eyes shining.

Hi, kiddo, the letter said in Mama's amused voice, starting right out as if they had talked just yesterday.

We're in San Francisco! Yes, all the way down here in California. And you'll never guess what's happened. I'm helping plan a nifty farewell party for those thousands of dolls going to Japan!

"She's in California," Lexie said aloud.

"I noticed the postmark. Did she get your letters?"

Lexie was already reading Mama's explanation.

Our old landlady forwarded your letters. I've kept every one, but gosh, I haven't had a minute to sit down and write. I've gotta rush now and get to practice.

But isn't it the cat's meow! You're up there earning pennies toward buying one doll for Japan and I'm down here planning to send them all off with a bang-up party. It's like we're working together.

No, Lexie thought. She wanted to crumple the letter but made herself smooth it on her knee instead. *It's not like that at all.* Not while she was here and Mama was way south in California.

There wasn't much more. Toby would be waking up soon, Mama had written, then they would be off to the speakeasy where he was playing with a band.

I'm their songbird, kiddo! I'm learning a piece called "The Blue-Eyed Doll." Have you heard of it? It's all the rage in Japan, where everybody's eyes are dark. It's about a celluloid doll arriving on a ship from America. I wonder if that's where the idea came from for the dolls your bunch is sending over.

I'll be singing the song at the farewell party here in San Francisco. It would be peachy if you could hear me, but I can't imagine your grandmother agreeing to make the trip.

Kisses, kisses, kiddo. Merry, Merry Christmas! Be sure to mind Grandma and Grandpa. And study hard in school so you will grow up to be a smarter girl than your mother!

A single tear slipped down Lexie's cheek and onto the perfumed paper. She slapped it away with her hand. Anger was better than sadness. She folded the letter and slid it into the envelope. When she was sure of her voice, she said, "Mama's going to help with the dolls' party in San Francisco before they all go to Japan."

"I expect that will suit her." Grandma turned to the stove. "Hurry and wash up. Supper's almost ready."

Lexie smelled chicken baking, but she wasn't hungry. She was remembering Louise and Alma. They had said that the girl who wrote the best letter would go to San Francisco to see the dolls off. Mama would be there!

I have to write the best letter. I need to be close to the doll. I need to hold Emily Grace, to feel her in my arms and pretend to talk to her. It's the only way I'll know what to say.

Miss Tompkins had taken the doll home — to the room she rented from Jack's mother. *Just next door.* It was probably there now. Ideas flew through Lexie's head.

"I'm going to change my school clothes," she said, and ran into the hall and up the stairs. In her bedroom, she quickly changed from her school dress to an everyday pinafore and pulled on her coat.

She threw open her window, thankful the rain had eased to a sprinkle, and crawled into the old cherry tree that brushed its wide branches against her house and against the Harmons' boardinghouse next door. She reached the trunk, wriggled around it, and started along a second branch. "Jack! Jack, open your window. I need to talk!"

Was he home? He had to be home. "Jack!"

His window rasped upward. Jack leaned out, brown hair tousled by a damp wind. "You sound like a cat stuck out there."

"Miss Tompkins brought the doll home with her."

"How long did it take you to figure that out?" His grin lit up his whole face.

This was no time to be angry with Jack. "Is she home now? Miss Tompkins?"

"Naw. She just came in long enough to leave the doll." His grin faded, as if he'd heard something in her voice that worried him. "Why?"

"You've got to sneak me into her room."

"Are you crazy? No one goes into the renters' rooms. Ma would have my hide."

"You owe me, Jack."

"Since when?" He began hauling down his window.

"Since the cookie," she said quickly. "People still call me Dog Breath."

He paused with the window halfway down. Laughter sparkled in his eyes. "How'd that cookie taste?"

"You owe me," Lexie said again.

Jack tugged on the window. Lexie crept closer along the branch. Teetering, she let go to hold both hands toward him. "I won't touch anything. I have to see Emily Grace. It's important! Please?"

He raised the window again, making shushing motions. "Cripes! They can hear you all over the neighborhood."

"I knew you were a scaredy-cat!"

She saw him starting to reconsider and added,

"There's going to be a contest. If I write the best letter, I get to go to San Francisco with Emily Grace. My mama's there, Jack! But, if you're too scared . . ."

He glanced to either side. "Come around to the back porch. Make it fast."

CHAPTER 3

Minutes later, Lexie stood with Jack in the carpeted hallway outside a plain paneled door. What she was about to do went against everything she had ever been taught. This wasn't like slipping into the classroom after school. That might have earned her a scolding. This could get her into a lot of trouble. But she had to do it.

Jack leaned against dark wainscoting nearby, looking nervous. He wasn't supposed to be upstairs in his mother's boardinghouse, except for in his own room, at the end of the hall.

Lexie shouldn't be here at all, but she didn't have a choice. Not in her heart. Only one thing mattered more than getting caught: being with Mama again. To do that, she had to write the best letter in the whole class. And to do that, she *had* to hold the doll, to *know* what the doll would say to those girls in Japan. It was the only way to write a letter that was better than anyone else's.

Still, getting caught wouldn't be fun. She glanced down the stairs at a rain-streaked window, feeling as rain-blurred as the glass while she gathered courage to open Miss Tompkins's door.

"Go on in," Jack demanded. "Or forget the doll!"

I have to do it, Lexie told herself again. *I have to.*

She smelled simmering beef and onions and knew Jack's mother was making stew for the boarders' supper. Miss Tompkins's room was right above the kitchen. Anyone walking around up here might be heard downstairs. Could she walk softly enough that Mrs. Harmon wouldn't hear her from the kitchen?

Someone in a nearby room turned on a radio, making her jump.

Jack rocked on the balls of his feet. "What are you waiting for?"

"If Miss Tompkins catches us . . ."

"She won't."

"Maybe the door's locked."

"Nobody locks doors here. I don't think there are even keys."

Lexie looked at the doorknob, remembering how Grandma was always watching for some sign of Mama to root out of her. Sneaking into Miss Tompkins's room was sure to be one of those signs.

"Why do you need the doll?" Jack added, sounding impatient. "She's not going to write the letter for you."

"I've only ever held my cloth doll, Annie, that my grandma made me for Christmas when I was little. I don't know what a store-bought doll would write in a letter. Annie's so soft and sweet and loving, she'd just say, 'Give me a hug!' A pretty store-bought doll like Emily Grace would say more. I know she would. I just don't know *what*!"

"Then don't be a baby!" Jack grabbed her hand and shoved it onto the knob.

Lexie snatched her hand away. "Miss Tompkins might be in there!"

"She went out. But she'll likely come back if you don't get a move on." He glanced down the stairs. "Better not let Ma catch us sneaking into a renter's room."

If she does, Lexie warned herself, *I'll never know*

what to say in the letter. I'll never get to Mama. She grabbed the knob. This time, she turned it.

Somehow she was inside the room without remembering taking the last forbidden step. Jack slipped in behind her and eased the door shut. For a moment, the entire room seemed to blur. Slowly, Lexie sorted everything out: a window over there, a neatly made bed to her right, a desk with a fringe-shaded lamp beside a large box. Her gaze stopped on the box. She knew that box.

She darted across the room and raised the lid. There was Emily Grace, with her friendly blue eyes and painted smile. "Just look at her," Lexie breathed. The ladies in the school parents' club had made the blue satin dress and gray wool traveling cape. They were perfect for her. Lexie set the lid aside and reached for the doll.

"You said you wouldn't touch anything," Jack said, adding quickly, "Are your hands clean?"

"Of course." But she checked them for dirt from the tree. Maybe she should just look at Emily Grace. No. That wouldn't be enough. She had to hold her.

She rubbed her hands on her pinafore to be sure, then gently lifted the doll from the box. Emily Grace had real hair in blond curls, not at all like

Lexie's growing-out brown bob. And the doll's arms and legs and head were made of a hard material, not like Annie, who was soft all over.

Lexie rocked her backward. The eyes closed and Emily Grace said, "Mama."

"Oh," Lexie said. "Did you ever see a prettier doll?"

"She's just a doll."

"Just a doll! She's . . . she's an ambassador, like Miss Tompkins said. She's going to Japan! Didn't you look at the map pulled down over the blackboard?"

"I looked. She's got a long way to travel."

Gold stars gleamed over three cities on the map they'd studied. Miss Tompkins had pasted one over Portland, Oregon, and another over San Francisco, California. She put the last star far across the Pacific Ocean, over the port city of Yokohama, in the island country of Japan. A steamship would carry the dolls all that way.

"It sounds crazy to me," Jack added. "Twelve thousand dolls . . . How can they bring peace?"

Lexie wasn't sure. When Grandpa had read his newspaper that morning, she'd heard him worry aloud about the Japanese military. Grandma had reminded him that the Japanese had helped the

Allies during the big war that ended in 1918. But Grandpa still frowned.

"Grandpa says the Japanese are looking to spread into China, where the British have interests," Lexie said, remembering. "He says if the Japanese try to push the British out of Hong Kong and Singapore, they'll be stirring up a hornets' nest."

Grandma had simply winked and said, "Your grandpa has a bad case of the doubts today. Pay him no mind." But Lexie couldn't help wondering. "What if we're sending Emily Grace straight into a war?"

"That's why the dolls are going, isn't it?" Jack asked. "They're supposed to make friends so there won't *be* a war." He moved closer to the door, listening. "Hurry up," he added in a whisper.

Lexie held Emily Grace close and looked into her blue eyes. Softly, she asked, "What should your letter say, Emily Grace? What do you want to tell those girls in Japan?"

Jack's hand hovered over the doorknob. "Are you through?"

Lexie studied the doll's face, almost believing that if she listened hard enough, she would hear Emily Grace's doll thoughts. "In a minute."

"Cripes!" Jack said. "That's the front door. I'll

bet it's . . . It is! It's Miss Tompkins. She just greeted Ma. She's coming up the stairs!"

He darted to Lexie, grabbed her arm, and hauled her toward the window. "The fire escape! Come on!"

He threw open the window and pushed her through. She clambered down the rust-roughened ladder, one hand skimming the rail while her feet flew from one step to another. Jack followed so fast, she was afraid he might knock her to the ground.

Then her feet hit wet grass. She wrenched away from the ladder and looked up through light rainfall at the window, glad to see that Jack had thought to close it.

"Cripes! Lexie! Why'd you bring her?"

"What?" She looked at Jack, then down. And felt as if he'd slammed the window again, this time right on top of her. She still cradled Emily Grace in one arm.

CHAPTER 4

The window flew open with a scraping sound that shot straight into Lexie. She hadn't felt so sick inside since Toby, the saxophone player Mama married, said he didn't want a kid around. Crying hadn't helped then and it wouldn't help now.

Biting her lip, she flattened against the wall, hoping to make herself invisible. She clutched her coat around Emily Grace to shield her from the rain. In her arms, the doll felt almost like a real child.

"Jack Harmon," Miss Tompkins shouted, "what are you doing down there?"

Jack shouted right back. "Ma told me to wash the windows."

Silently, Lexie cheered. *Fast thinking.*

Miss Tompkins's voice rose higher. "In the rain?"

He took off running. The teacher shouted after him, "You were peeping in my window, young man. I intend to speak to your mother!"

Miss Tompkins hasn't seen me in the late shadows, Lexie told herself. *I can creep along the house and get away.* But Jack had tried to help. She stepped out from the wall.

Her heart pounded even harder than it had in the schoolroom, but she found her voice and talked fast before she could change her mind. "It wasn't Jack, Miss Tompkins. It was me. I went into your room for Emily Grace. I just wanted to hold her. And I forgot and brought her down with me."

"Electra Lewis?" Miss Tompkins leaned out farther. "Is that the Friendship Doll? In this rain? Bring her inside at once!"

Lexie winced when the window slammed down.

She wanted to walk slowly, hoping the ground would open beneath her before she reached the porch, but she knew she needed to rush Emily Grace inside out of the rain. She wouldn't be in any less trouble for involving Jack. She would try to leave him out of it.

The ground did not open. She reached the porch and stepped reluctantly through the front door. Miss Tompkins waited in the upper hall. "Come up here at once!" She returned to her room, leaving the door open.

Lexie's steps dragged. She had to go up there, but how could she? Hesitating, she slid her fingers through the day's mail left for renters on a hall table. Another letter from Mama would make all the awfulness better. . . .

Make sense, she told herself. A letter for her would be next door, not here. And mama's letter today had been the only one in the whole three months she'd been here. Lexie glanced up the stairs. Her feet would not carry her one step closer. She trailed her fingers through strands of beads on a nearby lamp shade. She could leave the doll on the table and run back to Grandma's.

Then she remembered that the friendship letter could take her to Mama. She looked hungrily into Emily Grace's blue eyes. If only she could spend more time with the doll.

Silence from upstairs sounded worse than if the teacher had begun to yell. The stairs looked twice as high as before with that dangerous open door at the top. The longer she waited, the more trouble she was probably going to be in when she got upstairs.

Holding Emily Grace tightly to her, Lexie began to climb. She drew on every bit of courage she could find to push her feet up the last carpeted step and into the hallway.

Lexie hovered in the doorway while Miss Tompkins carried the doll to the light near the window of her room. "I'm disappointed in you, Electra," the teacher said. "Please come inside."

Had she hurt the doll? The fear made her queasy. With her gaze fixed on Emily Grace, Lexie forced herself to cross the room. "I didn't mean to get her wet."

Miss Tompkins turned Emily Grace over, taking painful minutes to inspect her. "Fortunately, her cape protected her gown." She used a handkerchief to blot rain from Emily Grace's golden curls, still springy beneath her hood.

Lexie swallowed hard. Was she going to be told never to come to school again? What would she say to her grandparents?

Grandma didn't think too much of the doll project to begin with. It had a hint of show business about it, she said with her dislike of Mama in her voice. All that collecting money and holding bake sales and cakewalks didn't sit right with Grandma. It had taken a lot of convincing, even with Grandpa's help, to get her to agree that Lexie could take part.

Grandpa learned a lot and had stories to tell from his work as a teller in a bank. But he didn't like arguments and usually stepped back when Grandma got upset. If Miss Tompkins told them about Lexie's sneaking into her room to hold the doll, Lexie couldn't hope for sympathy from either of her grandparents.

The teacher's voice broke into her worried thoughts. "I do not believe you have one whit of interest in the meaning of the Friendship Dolls."

"I do!" Lexie protested.

"Then tell me why children in this country are sending more than twelve thousand dolls to Japan."

Lexie knew why. Of course she did. A man who had taught in Japan for many years had returned to America worried about growing tension between the two countries. The old emperor was unwell, and like Grandpa, the man feared war might be coming. He knew that Japanese families celebrated a special dolls' day in March, and he thought that if the children in the two countries shared dolls, they would become friends. Then when they grew up, they wouldn't want to make war.

Words tumbled about in Lexie's head, but none made it past her tongue. She stared miserably at Emily Grace. How could she hope to write the letter when she couldn't even answer Miss Tompkins's question?

"Electra?"

Words burst out. "Mama and her new husband sleep in the daytime because they work at night. And he said he doesn't want a kid around, and Mama said I'd be better off with Grandma so I could go to the same school all the time, so please don't say I can't go to class anymore! Please!"

Tears slid down her face, even when she blinked hard and tried to stop them.

She couldn't see Miss Tompkins clearly through the tears, but she thought some of the angry red color faded from the teacher's face. Miss Tompkins placed the doll on the desk, then offered Lexie the rain-dampened handkerchief.

Lexie wiped her nose and fought back the tears. "I didn't mean to hurt her. I just wanted to know her better. I heard there's going to be a contest. If I write the best letter, I can go to San Francisco with the doll. And my mama will be there, singing in the good-bye program."

Sympathy flared briefly in the teacher's face.

Her voice sounded warmer, but her words remained schoolroom firm. "I believe you know you were very wrong to take the doll from my room. You should not have come in here without permission."

Lexie twisted the handkerchief in her fingers and stared in misery at Emily Grace. She knew she should not have taken the doll, even by accident. The doll's eyes were closed as she lay on the desk, as if even Emily Grace could not look at her.

Miss Tompkins drew a deep breath. For a long moment, she gazed through her window. Finally, she said without turning, "You do understand that you must be punished?"

"Yes." The word came out so softly, Lexie could hardly hear it.

"Come to school ten minutes early tomorrow," the teacher said. "We will discuss the matter then."

Discuss the matter? That was a teacher's way of saying, *I will tell you then what dreadful thing I have decided to do to you.*

Lexie tried to think of something to say that would make the punishment easier, but again words wouldn't come. She could only twist the handkerchief some more, then place it carefully on the table.

"You may go now," the teacher said. "You will

present yourself in class ten minutes early tomorrow, Electra. Do you understand?"

"Yes," Lexie breathed. "Yes, Miss Tompkins." She threw a last agonized look at Emily Grace, then turned to the door. There she paused to cry out, "I'm sorry!" before she ran down the stairs and out of the house.

As she fled across the lawn, Jack caught up with her. "What did she say?"

"I didn't tell her you helped." Lexie gasped for breath. "I said it was just me." She sensed his relief, but that was no comfort. She still had to face Grandma. In her mind, she repeated Miss Tompkins's scary promise that they would discuss the matter tomorrow.

CHAPTER 5

"Miss Tompkins might make you sit on the bench in front of the principal's office, where everyone can walk by and snicker," Jack said the next morning. Lexie wondered why he'd bothered walking to school with her so early. She couldn't tell if he was sorry she faced punishment or was looking forward to it.

Jack reached over and tugged her pink knitted scarf away from her face. "Did your grandma ask why you were leaving early?"

Lexie pulled the scarf back. "I said I had to be at school before class for a special project." That was true. She just didn't know yet what the special project would be. The thought made the oatmeal she had eaten for breakfast weigh like a rock in her stomach.

"She'll wonder when she sees you walking funny from the walloping the teacher gives you."

Lexie turned around and glared. "You're not helping, Jack."

"Relax. She'll probably just make you write a hundred times that you won't do it again."

"Who sneaked me into her room?"

Jack slanted his cap brim against the rain, smile fading. "Who carried the doll down the ladder?"

The thought of that sent a shiver through Lexie. She'd been too scared to think when Jack had shoved her at the window and rushed her down the fire escape. She should have put the doll in its box. She'd meant to, but everything had happened too fast.

The fear that had haunted her all night couldn't be held back any longer. "I don't care what the teacher says. As long as she doesn't tell me I can't go to school anymore. Mama's counting on me. So are Grandma and Grandpa."

Jack was silent. Maybe he was thinking it would be a good thing to have to stay home from school. It wouldn't be, though, not for her.

From down the street, a girl called, "Jack!"

Louise Wilkins ran to join them. She always looked like she'd stepped from one of Mama's fashion magazines. Today, she wore a side-belted coat with a matching cloche over her perfect bob. She smiled at Jack, then glanced at the space where Lexie walked beside him and, as usual, saw no one there.

"Hey, Louise," Jack said with enthusiasm that made Lexie wrinkle her nose in disgust.

"Papa helped me with the math homework." Louise sparkled up at Jack. "You can borrow it if you like."

"Why?" Lexie asked. "Don't you think he's smart enough to do it himself?"

Louise kept her smile aimed at Jack. "I think Jack can do anything he wants. And so can I! Look, I talked Papa into giving the class fifty cents for our doll. That is half the cost of her steamship ticket!"

Jack whistled softly.

Lexie pushed away resentment to say, "Louise, do you know if it's true about the letter contest winner getting to go to San Francisco?"

"I might know, but I won't tell!"

Lexie looked at the smug smile on Louise's face. If Louise thought she was going to beg for an answer, Louise was wrong.

In the same moment, a girl in the school yard called, "Louise!"

"See you later, Jack." Louise took a step away, then turned and for the first time looked directly at Lexie. "What do you care about the rumor? You're wasting your time. I'm writing the best letter. Mama said so!" She ran to join her friend.

Lexie thought of several things to say about Louise and swallowed them all. Grandma said the Wilkinses acted as if their money gave them special privileges. Maybe it did. And Mr. Wilkins was on the school board. Could that mean the judges would choose Louise's letter even if it wasn't the best?

Lexie had to believe that the judges would be fair and choose the best one, no matter who wrote it. And she was going to write the best letter. Not Louise.

As they reached the school, morning sunlight broke briefly through the clouds, brightening the white paint on the two-story building. From the green-wooded hillside beyond, the *rat-tat-tat* of a woodpecker sounded sharp in the early morning.

Lexie felt every tap in her heart. Whatever was to happen, it was time to face Miss Tompkins. Pulling her shoulders straight, she headed up the walk to the small covered porch.

"Lexie, listen," Jack began. "I've been thinking. . . ."

Lexie ran up the steps, shouting over her shoulder, "I can't be late."

The hall stretched ahead of her with classrooms to either side, looking strange without students laughing and jostling one another. Her steps sounded hollow on the wood floor as she walked alone to the sixth-grade classroom at the back. As she reached for the door handle, her heart pounded.

Since students weren't allowed inside yet, no one was crowded around the fat wood-burning stove at the back of the room. As much as Lexie would have liked to warm herself, she turned away. Miss Tompkins waited behind her desk near the blackboard at the head of the room. The distance from the door had never looked so great before. As Lexie walked toward her, she felt as if the aisle stretched longer and longer.

And then, as if time had snapped back, she was standing beside the teacher. Miss Tompkins looked up from the paper she had been reading. "Good morning, Electra. I am pleased to see you are on time."

"Yes, Miss Tompkins." Lexie's voice sounded

faint when she wanted to sound strong. She swallowed, ready to try again.

The teacher placed a leaflet on the desk. "Do you know what this is, Electra?"

Lexie read the heading. "It's about the kind of dolls to send to Japan."

"Correct. The Committee on World Friendship Among Children has listed several requirements for the dolls. I find we have failed to meet those requirements for Emily Grace."

"We have?" Lexie frowned at the leaflet. "How?"

Miss Tompkins flipped open a page. "Please read aloud, beginning with this paragraph."

Lexie drew in a breath. She didn't read as well as some of her classmates. Skipping around from school to school so Mama could find work singing with bands had made her slower.

Again, she straightened her shoulders. "It says, 'The dolls should be thirteen to sixteen inches tall and should look like attract . . . tive, typ . . . typical American girls.'"

"Good. Continue."

Lexie thought of Emily Grace and decided she was probably the right size and she was pretty. *Even prettier than Louise.* But Miss Tompkins hadn't said the doll looked wrong.

Lexie glanced at Miss Tompkins and began again. "It says, 'The dolls should be new and not cost more than three dollars.'" That sounded like a lot of money. She had heard Grandpa say the bank paid him twenty-five cents an hour. Still, the class had collected enough to buy the doll by selling cupcakes and holding a cakewalk at the school carnival.

She looked at the list again. "The face, arms, and legs should be of un . . . unbreak . . . able material. The . . . joints . . . and wigs should be hand sewn." She paused. "Emily Grace is right, isn't she, Miss Tompkins? She is those things."

"She is. You have not yet reached the problem."

Lexie glanced down the list. The dolls should be able to open and close their eyes and say "Mama." They should each have a letter. Her heart beat faster. Emily Grace's letter was going to be from her. It had to be.

"Electra? Are you having difficulty reading the list?"

"No, but I don't see a problem, Miss Tompkins. It says each doll must have a railway and steamer ticket for travel and a passport and visa. We're raising money for those."

She thought of the shiny fifty-cent piece in Louise's hand. "Is it about the money? Because——"

Miss Tompkins cut her off. "I do not expect difficulty with the money. You are skipping about, Electra. You have missed the one item I wished to hear you read."

Lexie glanced swiftly over the paper. This time, her gaze stopped at a paragraph in the middle of the page. Aloud, she read, "They should be . . . simply . . . and care . . . carefully dressed. Extra dresses are desire . . . desirable."

Heart sinking, she raised her eyes to the teacher. "Emily Grace has a pretty satin dress with ruffles, not a simple one."

"Nor does she have an extra dress," Miss Tompkins said. She clasped her hands together on her desk and gazed at Lexie.

The expectant look in the teacher's eyes made Lexie's thoughts race. "I could make a second dress for her!" And hold her and measure her and fit the dress to her. She held her breath, hardly daring to hope that Miss Tompkins would agree.

Punishment, she reminded herself. *It has to sound like punishment!* Aloud she added, "I wouldn't have time to play. I'd have to stay in after school every day to work on the dress."

It looked like a smile teased the corners of Miss Tompkins's lips, but Lexie couldn't imagine why.

"And I hope you will remember that your own reckless behavior brought the punishment upon you."

"I will!" Lexie said with all the promise she could load into her voice.

"Your assignment, then," the teacher said in a firm voice, "is to design and sew a simple second dress to place in the trunk to travel with Emily Grace to Japan."

Lexie suddenly remembered that she had never so much as hemmed a handkerchief! She didn't like to admit that she couldn't do something. But to sew a dress nice enough to travel with the doll to Japan might not be possible.

Heat rose to her cheeks. Everyone would laugh at whatever she managed to stitch together. Where would she even find material?

"You may ask your grandmother to help you." Miss Tompkins placed the leaflet in her desk drawer. "You have three weeks, Electra. Perhaps the next time you are tempted to go into a place where you do not belong, you will remember that actions have consequences."

"Yes, I will," Lexie said, but wondered if she'd made another mistake when she offered to do something important without knowing how. To ask for Grandma's help, she would have to admit that she had gone into the teacher's room to see the doll! Her thoughts spun so fast, she felt dizzy.

"You are dismissed," Miss Tompkins told her. "Please wait outside with the others for the class bell."

Feeling dazed, Lexie turned away and forced her steps toward the door.

"Electra."

She stopped at the teacher's call, then turned slowly, wondering if a second punishment was to be added to the first.

"You will need to take measurements and fit the dress to the doll. You may visit her in the boardinghouse when necessary, at any time when I am there."

She was to have all the time she needed to hold the doll, to get to know her. She would understand Emily Grace better than anyone in the class. She would learn exactly what to say in Emily Grace's letter.

"I will," she said. "I will, Miss Tompkins!" She felt as if she could do anything, even sew a dress worth traveling with Emily Grace to Japan. Even tell Grandma. Even ask for her help. She would find a way. Somehow. Feeling a smile light her up inside, she ran onto the school porch.

She ran right into Jack. "I've been waiting for you," he said, talking fast. "It isn't right. What happened was my fault, and I'm going to own up to it."

"No." She saw her chance with the doll slipping away. Making the dress was something she needed and wanted to do. What a time for Jack to decide to be a hero. She wished she hadn't said she was afraid of being sent away from school. He must have been thinking about that. "It was my idea. I made you take me to that room. I wanted to hold the doll."

Eyes bright, Jack reached for the doorknob. "I shouldn't have sneaked you in there. I'm not going to let you take the punishment. It was my fault, and that's what I'm going to tell Miss Tompkins."

"But Jack . . ."

He stepped inside as the bell rang, calling everyone to class.

"Jack, wait! It's not a punishment. . . ." As she started after him, others crowded through the doorway, shoving her aside.

"Jack!" she called over their heads. "I *want* to do it!"

He didn't turn around.

CHAPTER 6

Lexie wriggled into the classroom past two girls in the doorway comparing buckles on their shoes. She looked for Jack and saw him in the midst of a group of laughing boys.

In Lexie's mind, the doll slipped farther and farther from reach. If she interrupted while Jack talked with his friends, he was sure to make her the joke of his story. She felt cold inside just thinking how everyone in class would act if they learned she had sneaked into Miss Tompkins's room in the boardinghouse to see the doll. So she kept watching Jack, hoping he would feel her eyes on him and come over.

Miss Tompkins rang her handbell. As everyone settled into their seats, Jack eased into his desk across the aisle. Lexie leaned toward him, whispering, "Jack!"

He whispered back, "Don't worry!" and opened his desk to take out his math book. A warning glance from the teacher burned across Lexie, drying another whisper on her tongue.

As the morning dragged on, she wasn't able to concentrate on fractions. Instead, she tore a corner from her paper. In small letters, she wrote, *I don't want you to do it.*

She waited until the teacher turned to the blackboard before leaning across to put the folded paper on Jack's desk.

As he began to unfold it, Miss Tompkins turned. "Jack. Please stand and read your note aloud."

Lexie wanted to melt into the floor. She clenched her pencil so tightly in her fingers, she thought it might break. Jack was good at making up stories. Silently, she urged him to think fast.

He stood slowly, unfolded the note, and read aloud, " 'I don't want you to do it.' "

Someone giggled. Two others snickered. One boy laughed. Miss Tompkins asked, "Do what?"

Lexie stared at her hands, wishing herself

anywhere but here. Miss Tompkins must think they were planning something else.

"Kiss her," Jack answered the teacher. "She doesn't want me to."

Lexie's head shot up. She stared at him while her face began to burn. Several of the boys whooped, and all the girls began to whisper and giggle.

Louise called, "You can kiss *me*, Jack . . . in your dreams!"

"In my nightmares," Jack answered back.

The whooping and giggling got louder. Miss Tompkins rang her bell. "Class! That will be enough. Jack, you may move to this empty desk in front for the remainder of the day."

Her secret was still safe. Lexie knew she was going to face a lot of teasing. She didn't care. She was more worried that Jack might talk to Miss Tompkins and take the blame about Emily Grace. Looking hard at him, she tried to warn him in silence while he gathered his books and moved to the desk in front.

The rest of the morning blurred past. It wasn't possible to whisper to Jack. And from the front of the room, he could easily confess when Miss Tompkins dismissed them all for recess.

She hoped he understood her note. The dread

inside her said it wouldn't make a difference if he did.

At recess, she waited impatiently while Jack joked with friends at the front of the room. The girl who sat ahead of her turned around. "I didn't know you were sweet on Jack."

"I'm not!" The words burst from Lexie. They sounded too loud, as if she was trying to hide that she did care.

Someone else spoke to her. She had to turn to answer, which meant no longer keeping an eye on Jack or Miss Tompkins.

Finally, she saw him leaving the room with some of his friends. She hurried toward the door, but Louise stopped her with a hand on her arm. "Jack's *my* boyfriend, Dog Breath. Remember that!"

When you moved as often as Lexie had with Mama, you heard a lot of inventive name-calling. Before she could use one of those names to pay Louise back for "Dog Breath," her grandparents' faces, looking sad, came to mind.

So she answered with an amused voice she had heard Mama use. "Maybe you should ask Jack if *he* remembers."

Brushing past Louise, she left the classroom and

looked for Jack in the yard. He was with a group of boys watching another do tricks with a yo-yo. Lexie walked over. "Did you tell?"

"Who?" He glanced at her as if he'd forgotten the doll.

"Miss Tompkins!"

"Tell her what?" He turned back to the yo-yo.

Lexie almost smacked his shoulder. "You know what!"

"Oh, that."

Worry had been burning holes inside her all morning. "Jack! Did you tell?"

He gave an appreciative whistle. "That guy's good."

Lexie jerked his sleeve. "Jack?"

Finally, he turned his attention to her. "No, your note said not to. Why not?"

Relief washed through Lexie. "Because it's not like a punishment. All I have to do is sew another dress for Emily Grace."

Jack raised his eyebrows. "Do you know how?"

She might have felt insulted that he thought she couldn't do it, except that she wasn't sure she could. "I'll learn. And I'll get to measure Emily Grace and fit the dress on her while I'm making it. I'll get to know her, Jack. I need that chance!"

She took a big breath, then added, "If you take the blame, I won't get to know her."

Looking as if it didn't matter one way or the other, Jack turned back to the yo-yo. "Wow! Look at that!"

"Did you hear me?" Lexie demanded. Talking to Jack was like talking to a fence post.

He didn't take his attention from the yo-yo, but at last he agreed. "I won't say anything, if that's what you want."

Lexie felt eyes boring into her. It was the way she felt when she frowned over a sentence diagram and suddenly Miss Tompkins asked if she needed help. She glanced around and saw Louise glaring from a corner of the schoolhouse. Laughter bubbled up through Lexie, along with some of Mama's flapper breeze. Making sure Louise was still watching, she said, "You're a prince, Jack," and soundly kissed his cheek.

He looked at her as if she had lost her mind.

Ignoring whoops and whistles from the other boys, Lexie said, "See you around."

Then she walked directly past Louise to a group

of girls playing hopscotch and took her place at the end of the line. As she waited her turn to hop, she glanced at the other girls, studying the dresses they wore. Could she really design and sew a dress for Emily Grace?

I can, she told herself. Sewing the dress would be easy. The hard part was going to be asking Grandma for help.

When class started again, Lexie considered one girl's dress after another. Was a bow too fancy for the plain dress the doll needed? Should the material be flowered, or striped, or all one color? How were sleeves put on?

Miss Tompkins's voice broke in, dismissing class. With relief, Lexie gathered her books. But the teacher spoke over the shuffling sound of the others. "Electra, please remain in your seat."

Those were the first words from Miss Tompkins that Lexie had heard clearly all afternoon. That might have been the problem. She might have missed hearing the teacher call on her. Maybe she would have to stay after class and write a hundred times that she would pay attention.

It might be even worse. Maybe Miss Tompkins wanted to tell her she wouldn't be making a dress for Emily Grace after all.

As Jack followed the others from the room, he glanced at her with a look she couldn't decipher. Then Louise paused beside her. "Bet you're in trouble!" With a satisfied smile, she joined her friends in the doorway.

CHAPTER 7

Lexie's fingers curled into fists in her lap. She looked straight ahead at the blackboard, waiting for whatever was about to happen while the last of her classmates left the room.

Miss Tompkins motioned her forward. Feeling as if she pulled each step through clinging mud, Lexie walked slowly to the front of the room.

Miss Tompkins opened a drawer and lifted out the box holding the doll. "You will need to get started with your project. Three weeks is not a very long time."

"Yes, ma'am." Was she to measure the doll now? Here?

She looked for a measuring tape on the desk, but the teacher said, "Since I will be away this evening attending a meeting, you may keep Emily Grace over the weekend. Do I have your promise to keep her safe and return her on Monday morning?"

"Yes! Of course! I will." Lexie cradled the box in her arms, half fearing that Miss Tompkins would change her mind and snatch it back.

"I will," Lexie said again, clutching the box and doll close as she backed toward the door. She paused to glance again at the teacher. "I won't let her get in the rain or anything. I promise!"

Wait until Jack saw that she had Emily Grace for the entire weekend! She hoped he would meet her outside, but instead Louise caught up with her. "What's that?" she demanded, poking the box. "Is that our doll? Are you stealing her?"

Lexie ignored her and kept walking.

Louise stayed beside her, looking at the box with suspicion. Suddenly she reached over and pried open one end. "That *is* our doll! Miss Tompkins!"

Lexie jerked the box away, nearly spilling the doll. "I'm doing a special project."

"Does Miss Tompkins know about that? Does she know you have the doll?"

Her tone said that Miss Tompkins could not

know because she would never let Lexie remove the doll from the school. Lexie put as much scorn as she could manage into her voice. "It's her project. Of course she knows."

The look on Louise's face was almost worth all the worry Lexie had been through during the day.

"I don't believe you," Louise said. "What did you do to deserve a special project?"

Again Lexie thought of Mama and the way she faced down anyone who doubted her. "Maybe Miss Tompkins likes my work better than yours." Head high, she walked down the street toward Grandma and Grandpa's house.

Her confidence faded as she neared the front gate. All her doubts about setting in sleeves and making buttonholes rushed back. If she made a mess of this, she would never live down the taunts she would hear from the others. And a poorly made dress could not go with Emily Grace to Japan.

As she rested the box on the gatepost, Emily Grace said from inside it, "Mama!"

"Oh," Lexie whispered. "You want a new dress, don't you?"

She lifted the lid, and Emily Grace smiled up at her, the doll's blue eyes looking interested and happy. Lexie could almost hear her saying that she knew she was going to love the new dress. She would love it even more than the fancy dress the ladies had made, because Lexie would put her heart into making it.

"I can do it," Lexie told the doll. "Mama said we can do almost anything if we want it enough. And I really want to make the dress."

Gently, she touched Emily Grace's rosy cheek. She tried to picture the doll wearing the dress she would make. But the picture in her mind didn't work. Instead of a pretty dress, she saw lopsided sleeves and a collar where the two sides didn't match. Even if she could make a dress, what would she use for material?

There was only one answer. She had to tell Grandma what had happened from the very beginning and somehow convince her to help. Worry pooled in her stomach, but she marched up the stairs and into the front hall.

She found her grandma in the parlor, dusting furniture that already looked polished. Putting it off never made a bad thing better. "Grandma," she began, bracing herself to get the worst over with as fast as possible, "I have to tell you something."

"Not now, Lexie." Impatience crackled through Grandma's voice. "The ladies in my reading circle will be here tonight. Hurry upstairs and change your dress. I want you to sweep the front stairs and the walk."

For a moment, Lexie felt she had been given a chance to escape, but she had already decided against postponing her confession. She tried again. "Grandma, something happened and—"

"I said later!" Grandma tugged a chair away from the window and busily dusted the sill. "Why are you still standing there?"

Grandma wouldn't feel ready for the ladies until she had polished everything twice. This was not the time to upset her by admitting sneaking into Miss Tompkins's room and taking the doll. *I can make the dress by myself,* Lexie decided. *I know I can. Mama was right. I can do anything if I just try hard enough.*

She put the box with the doll on a hall stand, then hung her coat and scarf on a hook. Mama had given her the scarf before sending her to stay with Grandma and Grandpa. Lexie slid the soft pink wool through her fingers, thinking of girls she had seen wearing knit dresses. Maybe finding material for the doll's dress wasn't a problem after all.

With a cautious glance into the parlor, she hurried to the sewing cabinet at one side of the kitchen for a pair of scissors. Grandma's big treadle sewing machine hung inside the cabinet, turned wrong side up so the bottom made a flat table with a bowl of flowers on it. Lexie didn't know how to use the machine. She wasn't even sure how to turn it right side up and make it stay that way. But she was sure she could sew by hand.

The kitchen smelled of Grandma's spice cookies, tempting her. No. She needed to keep her mind on the doll dress.

The scissors were in a small drawer at one side of the cabinet. Near them, she found pins and needles in a pincushion and a spool of white thread. Pins would keep the dress pieces from shifting while she was sewing. She shoved them into her pocket, then carried everything upstairs to her room.

CHAPTER 8

Her soft doll, Annie, leaned against the pillow on the bed. Lexie put Emily Grace beside her. "Emily Grace is visiting," she told Annie. "Soon she will be sailing all the way to Japan."

After giving Emily Grace a gentle pat, she picked up the scarf. She held it against her cheek for a moment, remembering when Mama chose it for her. Perching on the side of the bed, she placed the soft wool over the doll. "Do you like the pink, Emily Grace? It matches your cheeks."

Lexie stretched the scarf on the bed and placed the doll with her feet over one end. Then she pulled the rest of the scarf over her to see how long it should be. Taking the scissors, she carefully cut off the extra length.

"There, Emily Grace. Now you just need a hole for your head. I'll sew up the sides and tie a ribbon around your middle. Look, Annie. Isn't she going to be pretty?"

A rattle against the window startled her into looking around. Was it hailing? No. Jack Harmon was in the cherry tree between their houses. That was his signal.

As she walked to the window, she saw Jack make a face and throw another twig against the glass.

She shoved the window open. "What?"

"You got me laughed at. Why'd you do that?"

For a moment, she couldn't think what he was talking about, then remembered kissing his cheek. If that was his worst problem, he was lucky. She stuck out her tongue, closed the window, and went back to the dolls.

He threw another twig, but she ignored him.

When she folded the scarf in half, the cut end looked ragged. "I'll sew a hem all the way around the bottom," she assured Emily Grace. "First, we need a hole for your head."

When she cut into the scarf, the scissors caught

in the knit. She pulled them loose and tried again. At last, the hole looked big enough. She held it up to check, stretching out the knit.

The stitches began running from the cut part on, leaving empty trails like ladders down the scarf. Lexie grabbed the wool to stop the runs, but the loops kept unknitting, like a row of dominos that kept right on falling.

When Grandma knit something, she complained of dropping stitches. With her heart sinking, Lexie realized this was what Grandma meant. Maybe she could weave the loops of yarn back through the ladders.

Laughter from outside the window startled her. She looked up and saw Jack peering in. She jerked the scarf against her chest, trying to hide her mistake. "Go away!"

"Lexie!" Grandma called from downstairs. "Don't forget to sweep that walk!"

Jack must have heard Grandma, too. He scrambled back along the branch.

"Coming!" Lexie ran to the window and pulled the blind down in case Jack came back. She shoved the ruined scarf beneath the mattress, then quickly pulled off her school dress and hung it in her closet.

She took a cotton dress from a peg, then paused to spread out the skirt. It was white with tiny blue blossoms all through it. "There's enough cloth in this to make a dress for you, Emily Grace. Do you like the flowers?"

Guilt nudged her, as if Jack had asked through the window if she should cut up the dress.

He wasn't there, but she answered anyway. "It's mine. If I want to give it to Emily Grace, I can."

"Lexie!" Grandma called again.

Lexie pulled on the cotton dress and ran down the stairs for the broom.

Supper was over, the dishes washed and put away, and tea and cookies set out before she could return to Emily Grace. By then, Grandma's friends were arriving at the door, some by motorcar and others on foot.

Lexie sat on her bed with Emily Grace on her lap and Annie propped against the pillow. "Listen, do you hear that big motor? That's Louise's mama in their fancy Packard. I guess Mr. Ford's cars aren't good enough for her."

She felt a little guilty for saying something unpleasant, but she was only repeating what she had heard Grandma say to Grandpa when he admired the shiny black Packard.

Emily Grace tilted backward. "Mama."

Lexie giggled. "That's right. Her mama likes to control everybody; that's what Grandma says. I suppose that's why Louise is so bossy."

She looked closely at Emily Grace. The doll couldn't say anything except "Mama," but she said much more with her eyes. Lexie hugged her and placed her on the bed.

"I hope you will like Japan. Miss Tompkins says that country is very different from ours. They sleep on mats on the floor and have paper screens for walls. I wonder how they keep secrets."

She shook her head, thinking she wouldn't like that, even if she didn't have secrets. "Today, we wrote poems called haiku," she told the doll. "They have just seventeen syllables and are often about nature and seasons. I wrote one for you, Emily Grace. It goes like this."

She repeated carefully for the doll:

"We feel cold inside.
Our doll must go to Japan.
New friends wait for her."

Gently, she touched Emily Grace's cheek. "Miss Tompkins says a haiku should make you feel something. My haiku makes me sad."

She shook her head, pushing away the sadness. "Let's get started on your new dress. First, we need to draw a pattern."

She slipped off the doll's cape and turned her over to unsnap the tiny closures behind her neck. Gently, she pulled the blue satin dress down the doll's body, easing her arms from the sleeves.

"What a pretty pink petticoat the ladies made for you. The girls in Japan will like your beautiful clothes. And you're going to have an extra dress!"

She studied the snap closure. "I saw some of those in the sewing machine drawer. I'll sew them in just like these."

She turned the satin dress inside out to see the seams. The ladies had used a sewing machine to make those tight stitches, but even if she figured out how to use Grandma's, that big machine was noisy.

Besides, people had used plain needles and thread to sew long before there were fancy machines. It would just take a bit longer.

Humming a song she remembered Mama

singing, Lexie shoved the braided rug to one side. Then she slipped off her flower-sprigged cotton dress and spread the skirt on the wood floor. In her underwear, she placed Emily Grace on the fabric. She dipped her pen in her inkwell and with careful strokes, began to outline the doll on the cloth.

CHAPTER 9

The ladies' laughter and talk came up the stairs to Lexie. Sometimes, Mrs. Wilkins's voice rose above the others, crisp and sharp. Grandma's voice sounded warmer. "I'm glad we don't live with Mrs. Wilkins," Lexie told Emily Grace and Annie while she cut two doll-size pieces from the skirt of her cotton dress.

Annie looked a little sad, lying halfway off the pillow. Lexie pulled her straight. "When I get done, Annie, I'll make a new dress for you, too. Emily Grace needs hers first, to take to Japan."

She worked with the tip of her tongue between her teeth, sewing the side seams while the ladies' voices rose and fell from downstairs. It took much longer than she'd expected, but at last the seams were done.

When she held the dress up, it didn't look exactly the way she had imagined it. Maybe it would look better when it was on Emily Grace.

She placed the dress against the doll, but sucked in her breath. The carefully stitched seams were on the outside, where the flowers were prettiest. If she turned the material to put the seams inside, the dress would look faded. If she put it on the doll with the pretty side out, those rough seams would show.

"I did it wrong!" Lexie flung the dress to the floor. Then she took a deep breath to catch hold of her temper. She'd seen both Grandma and Mama do that, and even Miss Tompkins. "I made a mistake," she told the doll. "I'll just pull out the stitches and start over."

It was a slow process. She hated having to do the same thing twice, but she forced herself to keep at it. Later, she heard the ladies saying good-bye, then the sound of their cars starting up and driving away.

Mrs. Wilkins's Packard backfired like a fire-cracker going off. Then the big car roared into the night. Lexie yawned. She was tired, but the two sides of the dress were finished at last, with the seams where they belonged.

Grandma spoke from the doorway, sounding shocked. "Child, what have you done to your dress?"

Guilt churned through Lexie. "I gave it to Emily Grace. She needs a new dress."

"So you cut up one of your own?" Grandma's mouth set in a tight line. Lexie thought she must have looked the same way herself after finding the seams on the wrong side. She hoped Grandma would catch hold of her temper, the way she had then.

Grandma crossed the room and held up the doll dress. "This will never fit that doll."

Lexie's breath came out in a rush. "It won't?"

"No, honey, it won't."

Honey? Grandma only called her honey when she was pleased with her. That didn't happen very often. It didn't feel right now, not with her dress on the floor with two holes cut in the skirt.

Grandma placed the dress on top of Emily Grace and pulled the sides down. "Do you see? The sides won't meet, front and back. She's not a flat paper doll. You should have used enough fabric to reach all the way around."

Tears crowded up inside Lexie. She thought of

the work she had done, sewing the seams and then taking them out and sewing them again. She swallowed the tears and made her voice strong. "I'll cut pieces to sew into each side. That will make it bigger."

In her mind, she saw the others in the class, especially Louise Wilkins, pointing to the extra pieces and snickering.

Grandma tsked her tongue. "I think we can do better than that." She looked at Lexie. "That is, if your teacher doesn't mind my helping."

"Oh, no," Lexie said quickly. "She won't mind. She said I could ask you to help." She thought fast, not understanding Grandma's offer but needing to make sure of it. "I'd be so happy if you helped me. Mama doesn't sew. So I don't know how to do it right."

The last of Grandma's doubts disappeared from her face. The set of her mouth said that with all Mama's singing and sleeping late, it was little wonder she didn't find time for sewing. Out loud, she said, "Well, it's high time you learn. You should have asked me right away and not cut up your own good dress."

"I tried," Lexie reminded her, "but you were busy."

"I was." Grandma sat on the bed beside her. "And you didn't feel you could wait. We'll sort this out. But I hope the next time you win a special honor from school, I won't have to hear the news from Eleanor Wilkins."

Lexie looked at the dress to keep her shock from her face. Honor? This wasn't an honor. How could Grandma think so?

Louise! Louise must have told her mother— complained, probably—that Lexie got special favors from the teacher. Now Grandma would have to hear the truth, and it would be even worse because she expected to hear something good.

Lexie swallowed hard, searching for words that would ease the way to the truth. The truth would be even harder now. How would Grandma feel to hear that the honor was really a punishment?

"So this is the doll that is going to Japan." Grandma picked up Emily Grace and leaned her backward. The doll's eyes closed. "Mama."

Grandma chuckled. "Fancy, isn't she? I expect your Annie there is feeling left out."

"I told her I'd make her a dress, too." That would mean cutting more holes in her own dress. And that first one hadn't worked out at all.

An idea rushed into her mind. "Annie's smaller.

Maybe this dress will fit her. And not be wasted." She looked hopefully at Grandma.

"Why don't we begin fresh?" Grandma patted Lexie's shoulder. "I have some yellow sprigged chintz set aside for kitchen curtains. I believe there's enough there to make dresses for two dolls."

Lexie hardly dared trust the happiness that welled up through her. "They'll be like sisters in the same dress, one here and one in Japan."

Grandma smiled and placed Emily Grace in Lexie's lap. "You must have done special work to earn the honor of dressing the doll." She sat on the bed beside Lexie. "Why don't you tell me about it?"

CHAPTER 10

The truth was about to ruin everything. Lexie wanted to run out of the house and keep running.

Grandma waited for an answer.

Carefully, Lexie said, "Miss Tompkins asked me to make a dress for Emily Grace."

"I understand that," Grandma said. "I'm interested in hearing why you were chosen for the honor."

There was that word again. *Honor.* Lexie's face got hot. What she had done felt even worse. Was there any way to tell Grandma about sneaking into the teacher's room that wouldn't make her mad?

"I could not believe the nerve of Eleanor Wilkins," Grandma went on. "She actually said her daughter must have misunderstood. It was not logical, she said — logical, mind you — that you should receive an honor before Louise!"

Lexie looked at the pride shining in Grandma's face. Her heart seemed to shrink inside her. Shrink and turn black. How could she possibly tell Grandma what had happened?

"Was it about Japan?" Grandma asked. "I suppose you are studying that country."

"Yes," Lexie said slowly. "Yes, we're learning all about Japan."

Grandma waited to hear more. Lexie looked at Emily Grace. The doll's friendly painted smile seemed to tell her to start with something Grandma would like to hear. The poem! Feeling grateful to Emily Grace, she said, "Today we learned how to write Japanese poems."

"That's nice." Grandma sounded more puzzled than pleased. "I expected to hear you made a report on the country. But poetry can be . . . interesting."

Lexie didn't think Grandma was much interested in poetry. She would rather keep busy in the kitchen than read, but she did have the book group that had met tonight. Maybe this would be something new to the ladies, something they would consider for next time.

"You could tell your book ladies about Japanese poems," she said, hoping for a way to avoid the trouble she felt coming. "They're called haiku. The poems."

"Hai-ku? I don't believe I've heard the word before." Grandma pursed her lips, then seemed to gather a smile. "You wrote the best one? That's quite an honor."

That word again. Lexie felt as if good and bad thoughts were pulling her in two directions. But she *had* written the haiku the teacher liked best. So it wasn't a lie to let Grandma be happy about that. "I wrote how I felt about Emily Grace."

"I would like to hear your poem. Do you have a copy?"

"I know it by heart. It's just seventeen syllables. That's what haiku poems are. Seventeen syllables in three lines. They're supposed to be about nature and feelings."

"Why don't you recite your poem for me?" Grandma sat back to listen.

Lexie closed her eyes for a moment, bringing the words to mind, then put Emily Grace on the bed and stood up. "It goes like this:

"We feel cold inside.
Our doll must go to Japan.
New friends wait for her."

The poem made Lexie sad again. She glanced at Emily Grace. Already, the doll felt as if it belonged to her. It would be hard to send her away to Japan.

"I see you have the best part of your mother," Grandma said. "What I know of her, she likes songs and singing."

Lexie wondered if Grandma thought that was a bad thing, but Grandma stood up and gave her a hug. "It's a pretty poem. I can hear you put your heart into it."

Now, Lexie told herself. *Now is the time to tell Grandma about taking the doll by accident.* "Grandma," she began.

"You just make sure it's the best parts of your mother you take," Grandma said, as if Lexie didn't have good sense after all.

Grandma would find a way to blame Mama for the accident with the doll. She always found a way to blame Mama, even when she didn't say it out loud. Lexie had seen the blame in her eyes. Resentment curled through her. Maybe she should wait a little longer to say what had really happened.

All through the weekend, she couldn't get away from knowing she had to tell Grandma the truth. But she couldn't find the right words or the right time to admit that she had taken the doll from the teacher's rented room without permission.

Her haiku said she felt cold inside. And she did.

As she started for school on Monday, Jack surprised her by catching up and walking with her. He pointed to the box with Emily Grace. "Who takes something that doesn't belong to them, and for punishment gets that same thing? Cripes! Who does that?"

Lexie thought she knew the answer. She thought Miss Tompkins had a kinder heart than she let on. When Miss Tompkins had heard about Mama and Toby and that Lexie needed to write the best letter so she could see Mama in San Francisco, the anger had left her face. She had understood then why Lexie needed to hold the doll. Would Grandma understand, too? Lexie was afraid to find out.

"So that's your punishment?" Jack's tone said he didn't believe it.

"I've never sewn anything before," Lexie told him. "I only have three weeks to work on it after school, and the dress has to be nice enough to go to Japan!" Her heart thudded. The other kids would never let her forget it if she ruined Emily Grace's second dress.

She didn't want to talk about that. "The letter is what's important," she told Jack. "It has to make the girls in Japan like Emily Grace." *And win the contest.*

"Why wouldn't they like her?"

"She'll be different, with her blue eyes and blond curls." Lexie frowned. "Maybe the letter should ask those girls to be nice."

Jack kicked a stone from the path. "Isn't that like saying they might *not* be nice?"

"Maybe the letter should say Emily Grace is bringing a hug from girls who want to be friends."

"Put that in along with your haiku and you'll have it done." He walked away to join friends throwing a ball over the school woodshed to a team on the other side. They whooped and laughed as he joined them. One made kissing sounds toward Lexie.

She wanted to tell Jack she liked his idea about putting the haiku in the letter. Now was not the time. Raising her chin, refusing to look at the whooping boys, she walked to the school porch to watch over Emily Grace in her box.

The school bell hadn't rung yet when shouts broke out on the playground. "It's a fight!" someone shouted, running toward a gathering crowd.

Louise glanced over as she came up the walk. "Boys."

Someone else yelled, "It's Oliver! And Jack!"

Jack! Lexie ran toward the crowd. She heard Jack shout, "Take it back!"

Oliver Johnson, a red-haired boy who sometimes offered to carry her books, yelled back, "You *luuve* her! Ow!"

Lexie stopped short. Loved who? Oh, no! That kiss! Could they be fighting because of the kiss? Jack was never going to forgive her.

The principal, Mr. Anderson, raced from the building.

"Hit him again!" someone yelled.

"You got him, Jack!" another shouted.

A third screamed, "Come on, Ollie!"

The shouting stopped as suddenly as it had started. The boys scattered as Mr. Anderson waded in. Moments later, he came past Lexie, towing Jack with one arm and Oliver with the other. Both boys were red faced, their shirts pulled loose and dusty. Blood oozed from Oliver's lip and reddened Jack's cheek.

As the principal hauled him toward the school, Jack looked straight at Lexie. The hard look on his face was one she had never seen before and never wanted to see again.

CHAPTER 11

Jack and Oliver arrived in class just after Miss Tompkins rang her bell, but she made them sit at the front on opposite sides of the room. There was no chance for Lexie to speak to Jack. She wasn't sure she wanted to.

He didn't want to talk to her. He made that clear at noon recess. She hated feeling responsible for his fight, especially when he kept rubbing his forehead as if it hurt. Ollie's swollen lip didn't bother her. He probably deserved it.

Since Jack was at the front of the room, he was one of the last to leave after school. When he saw Lexie waiting by the door, he snapped, "I'm not walking with you."

"Are you okay?"

"What's it to you?"

His head hurts. That's why he's mean, she told herself. "What was it about? The fight?"

His face flushed. "*Your* eye should be turning black, not mine. You took the doll from the teacher's room. This should be *your* punishment."

She hadn't expected that. "I *was* punished."

"Yeah. Punished. By getting to sew a dress. By getting to hold the doll, even take her home. You were punished, all right." He brushed past her and ran toward the street.

Lexie yelled after him, "At least I'm not dumb enough to get into a fight!"

Lexie couldn't stop feeling that it was her fault Jack was mad. She hoped he didn't get in trouble with his mother for fighting. After supper, she climbed into the tree between the two houses and threw twigs at his window. His blind was pulled all the way down. He didn't raise it, although she saw his shadow when he moved past. She also noticed that the window was open an inch at the bottom.

Leaning as near as she dared, she called, "Jack? Are you all right?"

No answer.

She threw another handful of twigs. When the blind stayed down, she gave up and crawled back to her room.

She hadn't told him to fight Oliver. And if he did want to fight, he should have known better than to do it at school. "Louise said it right," she muttered. "Boys!"

The dress was almost finished. Grandma kept her promise to help, and over the next three days, taught her to use the treadle sewing machine. That turned out to be even harder than Lexie expected and a lot harder than it looked. Her first practice scraps of material slipped and twisted under the needle. Her seams were so crooked, she wanted to hide them.

Grandma tsked her tongue but said only, "Never mind. It's all part of learning."

While they sat side by side at the machine, Lexie felt closer to Grandma than she ever had before. It confused her when she thought about it. She felt close to Grandma, but she wasn't friends with Jack anymore. It was easier to keep her mind on the sewing.

Rocking her feet on the treadle while her hands guided the material was like patting her head and rubbing her stomach at the same time. Threads tangled and broke. Bobbin thread snarled. Sometimes she pulled the fabric too fast and the stitches got too far apart. Just when she had it, the needle broke.

That sharp *snap!* went through Lexie almost as if the needle had poked her hand. "Oh! I broke it!"

"We have another." While Grandma unscrewed the tiny wheel and replaced the broken needle, she got a faraway look on her face. "Did I ever tell you about the first needle I broke?"

As they worked, Grandma told stories about her own first lessons on the treadle machine. She put her hand over Lexie's to help guide the fabric. She felt warm and comfortable, and Lexie liked hearing her stories.

Jack had avoided Lexie since the fight on Monday. She told herself she didn't care. If he didn't talk to her, he wouldn't play jokes on her, and that was just the way she wanted it.

On Friday, she hurried from school eager to finish the dress, but stopped in the hall. Grandma and Grandpa were talking in the kitchen. Mama always said eavesdroppers never heard good about themselves, but a sharp tone in Grandma's voice held Lexie in the doorway, listening.

"I have more common sense in my little finger than that woman has in her entire body," Grandma said, her voice rising. "It's not right to raise the child's hopes."

Grandpa answered more quietly. Lexie couldn't make out his words, but her breath caught when she heard her name. They *were* talking about her.

"Who would accompany her?" Grandma demanded. "She could not travel alone, and steamship tickets do not grow on trees."

Lexie's thoughts swirled. Steamship tickets . . . travel. The need to know more propelled her into the kitchen. "Have you heard from Mama?"

Grandpa glanced at Grandma. There was no gentleness on her face as she shoved an envelope into her apron pocket. "If a matter concerns you, young lady, you will know soon enough. Right now, I believe you have homework."

Lexie looked at Grandpa, hoping he would say something, but he simply picked up his newspaper and settled into his chair by the stove. *Later,* Lexie decided, watching Grandma busy herself at the table with the envelope still in her pocket. *I'll ask her again when she's in a better mood.*

That night, she dreamed letters flew about her, just out of reach. She grabbed for them, but they fluttered from the tips of her fingers while Mama's voice laughed lightly from their folds.

The chance to ask about the letter crammed into Grandma's pocket never quite came. Grandma kept busy and kept Lexie busy. Grandpa's thoughts seemed always on his work at the bank.

Grandma helped set sleeves into the doll's dress and make a sash of contrasting blue. There was enough of the blue material to make a matching collar. After supper on Sunday, Lexie sat at the kitchen table, hand-sewing the hem with tiny stitches because Grandma said machine stitches would show.

The brassy sound of big-band music curled around the room from Grandpa's radio. He rocked in his chair near the cookstove, reading his newspaper. Nearby, Grandma worked on her ironing. A tempting smell of cinnamon apples from a pie set out for later scented the room along with the warm smell of freshly ironed cotton.

We're a family, Lexie thought, almost surprised. *We really feel like a family at last.*

Now might be the right time to explain about

needing to hold the doll and accidentally taking her down the ladder. Lexie turned words in her head, trying to choose the ones that would make Grandma and Grandpa understand. She still had to ask about the letter from Mama. Which should she do first?

She took a solid grip on her courage. "Grandma . . ."

The front doorbell jangled. Relief rushed through Lexie, but she ground her teeth. Now that she felt ready to go ahead and explain everything, she wanted to get it over with.

Grandma set her iron on its metal stand and walked into the hallway to the front door. Voices came to Lexie. She recognized Mrs. Wilkins's sharp tone.

Something about it made Lexie lower the doll dress to her lap. She noticed Grandpa look up from his newspaper. Then Mrs. Wilkins said clearly, "That's what Louise heard from Jack. I just thought you should know."

Jack! As a sharp sense of betrayal stabbed her, Lexie heard the door close. Grandma came into the kitchen with her eyes snapping. "I have received distressing information. Electra, I believe you have something to tell us."

Resistance tore through Lexie, feeling even deeper than her disappointment in Jack. She knew that expression. Grandma had already made up her mind to think something bad. She had probably found a way to blame Mama, too. Lexie bent over the doll dress, forcing her needle to take tiny stitches in the hem, refusing to think about anything but the stitches.

"Electra?"

It was like Mama's letter. Grandma had made up her mind not to share, even when the letter was clearly about Lexie. She hadn't listened when Lexie tried to tell her about the accident with the doll because she was busy cleaning for her book club ladies. Now it was too late. Her mind was set.

"Do not ignore me, young lady."

"What difference does it make?" Lexie muttered.

Grandma moved one step closer. "My own mother never put up with muttering from young people old enough to speak clearly. Let me hear you, Electra. What do you have to say for yourself?"

Lexie raised her head, pain making her angrier. Why didn't Grandpa say something? He never questioned Grandma, as if she were ruler of the household. Papa was like that, too. He had laughed at Mama sometimes, but he never said she was wrong.

This was why. He'd learned how to keep peace from Grandpa. No help would be coming.

Silence forced Lexie to speak. "You've already decided I'm wrong."

She glanced at Grandma in time to see a strained look cross her face. Lexie felt her body grow tight in defense.

They'd been so friendly together, like a family. Now everything had changed, and deep inside, she knew it was her fault for taking the doll from Miss Tompkins's room.

"Do you hear yourself?" Grandma demanded. "In my day, a flippant answer was not tolerated. But you get that from your mother."

Lexie lurched to her feet, glad to aim the hurt away from herself. "I knew you would blame Mama! You always blame Mama! But my mama would never listen to a lady saying mean things at the door. She would shut the door in her face!"

As Grandma drew in a sharp breath, Grandpa set his paper on the table and got to his feet. He stepped behind Lexie and placed his hands on her shoulders. "Sophie, give the child a chance to tell her side of the matter."

"That is exactly what I am trying to do." Grandma visibly controlled her temper, though her cheeks had become bright pink. "I will ask you again, Electra. What happened at the Harmons' boardinghouse with that doll meant for Japan?"

An ache spread through Lexie, blurring her thoughts and stabbing her heart. All she really knew was how desperately she missed Mama. Grandma blamed Mama for everything. It wasn't fair.

Feeling defiance flare inside her, she raised her head. "You aren't my mama. I don't have to tell you anything."

Grandpa's hands tightened on her shoulders, as if in warning. Too late. The words were out. And she wasn't sorry. She'd been sorry enough.

With her eyes too bright, Grandma walked over to the cookstove. "We are happy to have you with us, Electra, but you will not grow up to be as heedless as your mother. Not if I have anything to say about it, and I believe I do."

She shoved the lid lifter under the heavy stove lid and pulled it to one side. "To lead me to believe that sewing the doll's dress was an honor was a lie of omission. To my mind, that is no better than a lie spoken." Flames leaped from the wood burning in the open firebox. Grandma's voice snapped like the sparks. "Bring that dress over here."

CHAPTER 12

Shock washed the feeling from Lexie's face and arms to somewhere deep inside. All the resistance left her. Grandma couldn't . . . She *couldn't* mean to burn Emily Grace's dress. "But . . . it's almost done."

Sounding far away, Grandpa protested. "Sophie?"

Lexie hesitated, hoping Grandpa would somehow make things right.

Grandma raised the cast-iron lid higher. The fire burning below made a wavering glow on the surface. "A hard lesson is a lesson well learned."

Lexie held up the dress, as if it could change Grandma's mind. "See . . . ? The stitches barely show."

"Drop it in here."

Lexie's fingers clenched over the pretty flower-sprigged dress with its blue-trimmed collar and matching sash. She thought of all the tiny stitches she had hand-sewn into it. Miss Tompkins would be impressed.

But Miss Tompkins was never going to see it.

"Electra."

"I was going to borrow Emily Grace to try the dress on her. Miss Tompkins said I could."

Without seeming to move her lips, Grandma asked, "Did you hear what I said?"

Angry tears burned down Lexie's cheeks. She twisted around to look up at Grandpa but saw no rescue, though his face looked troubled.

Pride rushed new heat through Lexie's chilled body. She could be as strong as Grandma. She *was* as strong. But until she got to San Francisco, she had to do as Grandma and Grandpa told her. Even when she knew they were wrong. Lurching to her feet, she held the dress before her and tried to see it as nothing but firewood.

Grief could wait. Her entire body felt stiff with the feelings she locked inside as she crossed the kitchen to the cookstove. She didn't hesitate. She didn't dare. Her courage might not last.

She brought the dress over the open stove, held it briefly — in case Grandma had an unlikely change of heart — then opened her fingers and let it fall.

For a moment, the flower-sprigged cotton lay on the burning wood. Lexie nearly reached in to snatch it back. The cloth caught fire. Flames leaped. Grandma wasn't finished. "Bring the pattern."

"Surely she's done enough," Grandpa said.

Both Lexie and Grandma paid him no mind. Anger rode over anguish within Lexie, driving her to the sewing cabinet. She pulled open one of the small drawers and jerked the folded paper pattern pieces from under the scissors.

For a moment, she thought of the care she had taken in measuring Emily Grace. But that reminded her of the closeness she had briefly shared with her grandparents, and there was no room in her heart for closeness. She crumpled the paper pattern, carried it to the stove, and dropped it onto the burning cloth.

Grandma shoved the cast-iron lid in place. "Go on to bed. Think about the importance of honesty."

Lexie ran up the stairs, slammed her door behind her, and hurled herself onto the bed, sobbing into Annie's soft cloth body for the loss of the dress she had worked so hard to make. Even deeper sobs tore at her for the loss of the family closeness she had felt so briefly. "I should have told. Annie, I ruined everything!"

She wouldn't stay here. She would go to Mama. She would walk all the way to California. One step in front of the other for long enough would carry her anywhere.

Maybe I'll go to Japan with Emily Grace. They'll be sorry then. Or maybe they won't be. Maybe they'll forget me and ask each other, "That girl who was here . . . What was her name? Do you remember?"

Through the window, she saw a light go on in Jack's room on the far side of the old tree. *This is all Jack's fault. He must have told Louise. How else could she know?*

Anger blazed again, and she slid off the bed and climbed through the window and onto the tree branch. She crawled along the branch and gathered a handful of twigs. When she had crept as close as she could to Jack's window, she threw them, one after another.

He raised the blind and shoved open the window. "What do you want?"

"To tell you that you can be happy now. I'm

paid back. Louise told her mother about the doll and she told Grandma and now Grandma hates me!"

"Louise? How'd she know?"

"How'd she know? You told her. Her mother said so. I heard her."

"You dumb Dora. I didn't tell her. You oughta know me better than that."

"Then who did?"

"Nobody. Louise probably heard us arguing after school that day. She's a sneak. She was probably listening."

"If you knew that, you shouldn't have said anything."

"You were the one who insisted on talking about the fight with Ollie. The whole story came out. Remember?"

She did remember. And she knew he was right. He'd said she should be punished and she'd said she was and he'd said sewing a dress wasn't punishment. Louise must have heard it all.

Before she could say she was sorry for blaming him, Jack slammed down the window and closed the blind. Lexie reached for another twig, then changed her mind and crawled along the branch back to her room.

She wanted to stay angry. She needed to stay angry, but slowly her earlier words to Annie spread through her. She'd been wrong to accuse Jack. And she should have told Grandma at once about the accident with the doll. Downstairs, she should have tried to explain instead of clamping the truth away just because she hurt inside.

Maybe it wasn't too late. Maybe she could go down and apologize. Then she could start over and tell what happened from the beginning and why she couldn't stop it once it got started and how Louise had taken it into her head that making a dress for Emily Grace was an honor.

She tiptoed down the stairs, trying words in her head, pushing away any that tempted her to make things sound better for herself. She would tell it exactly the way it had happened. At the bottom of the stairs, she paused as she had when Grandma and Grandpa talked about the letter from Mama. They were talking now. About her.

CHAPTER 13

You may be right." Grandma sounded tired, making guilt stab into Lexie as she listened from the stairs. "I may have been too harsh, but she's a smart child, growing up faster than we want to see. She needs guidance."

"She'll receive guidance," Grandpa said gently. Lexie pictured him rubbing Grandma's hand the way he sometimes did when she was upset. "We must be sure to temper guidance with love, Sophie."

"Of course I love her," Grandma exclaimed, sounding insulted. "But when I look at her, I see her mother and I think of the outlandish choices that woman has made. Look where those choices led her. . . . Singing in nightclubs, and who knows what goes on there."

"We won't imagine what we don't know," Grandpa warned.

Grandma sighed so loudly that the sound carried to Lexie on the stairs. "We know she insisted on buying a fancy motorcar that carried our son to his death."

Lexie couldn't listen any longer. She ran back up the stairs, careful to make no sound. Grandma blamed Mama for Papa dying in the motorcar crash. *That's reason enough for Grandma to lock away tender feelings when she sees anything of Mama coming out in me.*

As she climbed onto her bed, Lexie felt more confused than before. Slowly, she let her body sink into the covers while she hugged Annie.

Much later, a soft knock on her door startled her awake. She sat up, brushing her cheeks with her palms.

"Lexie, honey?" Grandpa asked. "May I come in for a moment?"

"Okay." She swung her feet from the bed and sat up.

Grandpa left the door open and settled into a

chair near her. "I was just thinking, honey. Rain clouds and stormy moods take time to blow away, but sooner or later the sun always comes out."

Lexie looked into his troubled eyes, trying to understand what he meant.

He leaned toward her, his hands on his knees. "She'll get over her crossness, you know, your grandma."

Reaching behind her, Lexie pulled Annie onto her lap. "No. I don't think she will."

"Grandma loves you," Grandpa said. "We both do. But she's a woman who sees things in black and white. And there's bad blood between her and Eleanor Wilkins, has been for a long time."

Lexie hugged Annie closer. Grandma and Louise's mama could fight it out in the middle of town, as long as they left her alone.

Grandpa pushed one hand through his thinning hair. "Tonight, your grandma feels . . . Well, she feels a little of the way you're feeling: betrayed, disappointed . . . pulling back to a safer place. It's a big responsibility to raise a little girl. Sometimes the more you love her, the harder it is because you want so much for that girl to grow into a sensible and happy young woman."

"She made me burn the dress," Lexie said into Annie, all the pain of that moment rushing back into her.

"She was feeling proud of her granddaughter in front of her friends, especially Eleanor Wilkins," Grandpa said. "Now she feels let down and maybe embarrassed. That's a hard thing for her."

"It's harder on me," Lexie protested, but her voice sounded small. She took a deep breath. "I didn't mean to take Emily Grace from Miss Tompkins's room. But I *had* to hold her. I had to know her, to know what to write in the letter that's going with her. Because the best letter writer gets to go to San Francisco. And Mama's there."

She took another deep breath before finishing in a rush. "And it was an accident because Miss Tompkins came back and Jack said to go down the fire escape and we did and I still had Emily Grace in one arm. So then I had to take her back to Miss Tompkins and say why I had her."

Grandpa leaned over to put one hand over hers, warm and comforting. "You told Miss Tompkins the truth. That wasn't an easy thing to do."

"No. And Grandma was busy getting ready for her book ladies. And then . . . there just wasn't another time to tell her." Tears blurred her eyes.

She stared down at Grandpa's hand over hers. "And I guess Louise heard Jack and me talking about it and told her mother and now Grandma hates me."

"No, honey. We both love you. We always will. Nothing can change that."

There was never going to be a better time to ask the question that had been burning inside her for days. She couldn't bottle it up anymore. "Did a letter come from Mama? Does she want me to go to her?"

Grandpa's hand tightened over hers almost as if he'd felt a stab of pain. "Honey, your mama doesn't always think things through. Sometimes the things we want just aren't possible."

"But it is possible, Grandpa! I'll be safe on a steamship. I won't leave my cabin. Not until we get there. I promise!"

He reached out to pat her shoulder. "You're safe here. Believe me when I say we love you and want you with us. I'll talk to Grandma. This . . . little storm will blow over. That's my promise."

"But . . ."

"I'll tell you what," Grandpa said, getting to his feet. "You get a good night's sleep. Then Monday after school, you come by the bank. We'll go next door for a dish of ice cream, just the two of us."

A ragged breath shook through Lexie. She wasn't done asking questions, but they would have to wait. So she simply asked, "Chocolate?"

Grandpa chuckled. "You can have all the chocolate ice cream you want. And after that, I have a friend I want you to meet. She may have a surprise for you."

He paused at the door, reminding her as he sometimes did of her papa. It was in the way he smiled with a sparkle in his eyes that spread over his face. "Things will look better tomorrow. That's another promise. Good night, honey."

"Good night," she answered softly. While his steps faded on the stairs, she sat with Annie and tried to think through everything that had happened. She had made a mistake to keep the truth to herself for so long. She would tell Grandma she realized that and was sorry she hadn't explained sooner. Part of her rebelled at the thought of apologizing. Grandma said Mama hadn't grown up right. She saw things she didn't like about Mama when she looked at Lexie.

"That's not fair," Lexie whispered to Annie. "She doesn't give me a chance to be me." But then she remembered Grandpa talking about it being hard to raise a girl, especially when you loved her.

They didn't know her very well. When they did, they would learn that she made good decisions. Most of the time.

A sigh almost as heavy as Grandma's made its way through her, and she decided not to worry about it anymore tonight. After changing into her nightgown, she pulled Annie close again. "I've never been inside the ice-cream parlor," she told the doll. "But I looked through the window one day. It has round tables, and when the door opened, I could smell sweet syrups."

Maybe she wouldn't start walking to California just yet. At least not until after the ice cream and Grandpa's surprise. And more questions about that letter she'd seen Grandma push into her apron pocket.

CHAPTER 14

When Lexie stepped into the ice-cream parlor with Grandpa on Monday, every surface gleamed, inviting customers with chocolate- and strawberry-colored paint. It was a magical place that made her mouth water with anticipation.

Grandma had made oatmeal that morning with brown sugar on top with the milk. Lexie knew it was a way of saying she was sorry about last night. Sometimes, words were hard for Grandma, the way they were for her.

Feeling a need to say she was sorry right back, Lexie had hugged her before running to school. Grandma had hugged her, too, and later,

Lexie found a freshly baked oatmeal cookie in her lunch box.

Now Grandpa swept out a chair with a round seat and a heart-shaped back and waved her onto it. Each table held a Christmassy red candle standing upright in an ice-cream sundae dish, with little gold balls around it. While Lexie slipped her arms from her cloth coat and hung it over the chair, Grandpa placed his hat on an empty chair between them. Lexie looked around, trying not to think of missing Mama at Christmas. "It smells good in here, like . . . strawberry and chocolate and umm, caramel."

A curly-haired waitress with a frilly apron came to their table, smiling. "We'll have two of your finest ice-cream sundaes," Grandpa told her. "Don't spare the whipped cream and remember to put a cherry on the top!"

"Coming right up." The waitress whisked behind a long marble-topped counter. Lexie heard a metal scoop clatter against a bucket.

She saw the ice-cream sundaes listed on a board behind the soda fountain and was shocked to see how much they cost. When Grandpa had said she could have chocolate, she expected a nickel scoop of ice cream in a dish. Did Grandma know that

Grandpa would spend fifteen cents on one ice-cream sundae? And he got one for each of them. He would have to work a whole hour to earn that much and still not have quite enough.

Minutes later, when the waitress brought the sundaes, Lexie forgot to worry about how much they cost. "They're beautiful," she breathed.

Each boat-shaped dish held scoops of vanilla and chocolate ice cream beneath thick blankets of chocolate syrup and creamy marshmallow sauce. Mounds of whipped cream rose on top, with a juicy red maraschino cherry at the very peak. Crunchy cookies poked like wings from each side.

The waitress beamed. "Enjoy it, honey."

Lexie carefully lifted the cherry with her spoon and put it into her mouth. It tasted as good as it looked. She decided to eat her sundae slowly, so it would last as long as possible. Secretly she hoped somebody from school would come by and see her there with Grandpa and the ice-cream sundaes.

"Next time," Grandpa said, raising his spoon, "we'll invite Jack from next door. You might like someone of your own age to talk to."

"I like talking to you." Lexie hesitated, then added, "Besides, Jack hates me."

Grandpa lowered his spoon. "Hates you? Since when?"

Since I kissed him and he got teased and got into a fight and blames me, Lexie thought, but said only, "He just does."

"I doubt that." Grandpa turned his attention to his ice cream.

Lexie churned her chocolate into slush, frowning at her spoon. "He won't talk to me. He calls me a dumb Dora and knocks into me when he passes in the hall. Or pretends I'm not there."

Grandpa let a spoonful of ice cream melt in his mouth for a moment. Finally he said, "Boys have trouble figuring out how to treat girls they like. I expect he's just sweet on you."

Lexie shook her head. Grandpa hadn't seen the way Jack turned away when she spoke to him or how he made sure they didn't walk together anymore.

"Well," Grandpa said after another long moment, "tell me this. How's that doll's letter coming along?"

All her hopes for the letter rushed into her mind. She felt she knew Emily Grace much better now. Losing the dress hurt like a wound that wouldn't heal. That made the letter even more important.

No one had said anything more about the winner of the contest going to San Francisco. Maybe it was a secret. Louise had said so. Maybe it wasn't even true. Lexie pushed that thought away.

She was glad that Grandpa hadn't mentioned the burned dress. She wasn't sure she could talk about it. Grandpa must feel the same way. Would he talk about the letter from Mama?

She scooped up some marshmallow cream while she thought about asking more questions, but she didn't want to spoil this day. She let her questions go for now and answered Grandpa's. "I wrote a Japanese poem. It's called a haiku. I'm thinking of putting it in the doll's letter."

"Sounds like a bang-up idea."

Lexie thought of the snappy flapper words Mama loved to use. For a moment, the familiar ache caught her. That letter from Mama must say she should come for a visit. Or to stay. Still thinking about Mama, she joked about adding her poem to the doll's letter, "It will be the cat's meow."

Grandpa chuckled. "Or the cat's whiskers."

Grinning, Lexie added, "Or the cat's kimono!"

Grandpa laughed and tapped his water glass to hers. "The winner!"

Still smiling, Lexie dug into her ice cream.

It was the best she had ever tasted. Her time with Grandpa flew by. Again, his twinkling eyes reminded her of Papa. He motioned the waitress over and paid the bill, then stood and reached for Lexie's coat. "On to the surprise!"

Lexie looked around, wondering if the surprise was another kind of ice cream and thinking she couldn't eat anything more. Maybe Mama was here! She knew that wasn't likely. Still, hope soared higher as she looked past Grandpa.

He opened the door with a flourish, snapped his hat over his head, and waved her onto the rainy wood sidewalk. "You're going to meet one of my favorite customers from the bank. I talked to her this morning, and she's expecting us. She goes by the name Mam'selle Maxine in her shop, but she's really just Maxine Fields from over on the coast, where her father's a logger."

Lexie raised her collar against the rain. "Why is she called Mam'selle? Isn't that French?"

"It is and that's her secret. Those who know go along with it, and those who don't know are impressed. It's good for her business."

"Her business?"

"Ah, that's my secret. Are you ready? Her shop is on the next street. It takes up her front parlor."

Lexie's mind whirled as she tried to imagine who the lady might be. Maybe she wrote letters for people who couldn't get their thoughts to come out the way they wanted. Maybe she was going to help with the letter. Maybe she had lots of pretty papers in her shop. And colored inks.

The papers and inks would be good, Lexie decided, *but I need to write my own letter. It has to be exactly what Emily Grace wants to say.*

Her thoughts rushed on, each stumbling over the next. *If Grandpa found a lady to write the letter, what should I say to her? I don't want Grandpa to feel bad. He means to help. And I need him in a good mood so I can ask about the letter Grandma shoved in her apron pocket that day.*

"Here we are." Grandpa stopped before a neat house with gingerbread trim around the front porch. A lace-trimmed sign in the front window read MODISTE in lavender script.

As they stepped inside, a string of little bells jangled overhead.

CHAPTER 15

There were no racks of fancy papers. Instead, shelves shimmered with folded fabrics. At one side, a headless dress form wore a smart frock of Christmassy green. Tapered sleeves hung empty.

A woman knelt before the form, her mouth clamped over pins she was working into the hem of the green dress. Her blond hair curled in glossy waves over her ears. Mama would have approved of her hairstyle and the straight cream-colored dress that flared over her legs. A rope of pearls swung forward while she worked.

When the bells jangled, she looked up, spit the pins into her cupped palm, and stood up, smiling.

After dropping the pins onto a nearby ironing board, she came to them with both hands outstretched.

"Ah, this will be the small Electra! You bring the sunshine on this cloudy day. Welcome!"

"This is Electra," Grandpa agreed. "Lexie, meet Mam'selle Maxine."

"So enchanting!" Mam'selle rushed on. "Grandpapa talks often of his little Electra who has come to stay with him and her grandmama."

Lexie looked from her hands to the woman's smiling eyes. For a moment, she felt overwhelmed. Then she remembered that Mam'selle Maxine was not really French. The visit became a game.

Instead of backing away, she said, "I like your shop, Mam'selle."

"I believe you will soon like it even better." Dimples appeared in the woman's cheeks. Pearls swinging, she tugged Lexie toward a table heaped with magazines. "Grandpapa has talked of the dress you would make for a doll. Let us look at fashions to suit her, yes?"

The seamstress sparkled and talked as she turned pages. Lexie was surprised she had been quiet with pins in her mouth when they first came in. She seemed to be making up for it as she exclaimed over pictures in the fashion magazines, pointing out bows and pleats and ruffles.

When Lexie finally got a word in, she said, "It has to be a dress for everyday. Emily Grace — the doll — already has a fancy one."

"Ah, too bad. We would have enjoyed the ruffles. But no matter. We will find just the right dress. This, perhaps? Notice the dropped waistline and the bow at the back with trailing ribbons from the waist to the hem."

"I think the sleeves would be hard to set in," Lexie said doubtfully, remembering the problems she had had before.

"But you have a modiste to help you, *petite*. We will set in the sleeves and pleat the bodice just so. And the neckline . . ."

She continued talking, but Lexie stopped listening. At first, relief had swept through her. Emily Grace would have her second dress. She had turned a grateful smile toward Grandpa as he settled onto a chair to wait.

But now she heard Mam'selle Maxine talking about pleats again. She sounded as if she would make the dress herself. *I'll be lucky if she lets me cut out the pieces,* Lexie thought, her joy changing into disappointment. She remembered her worry about letting someone else write the letter . . . and about hurting Grandpa's feelings.

"So let us begin," Mam'selle exclaimed. "Where is the doll? We must have her measurements."

"Umm, I know them," Lexie said. "I measured her before. I remember."

"*Bon.* You trust your memory, yes?"

"Yes," Lexie said. "But . . ."

"I think cotton poplin," Mam'selle said, rushing to a shelf and thumbing through a stack of folded fabrics. She pulled out a pink length with narrow violet stripes. "This, perhaps?" With a satisfied smile, she added, "I will display the little dress in my window. Until it becomes time for the costume to travel with Emily Grace to Japan."

Lexie glanced at Grandpa. He sat back, smiling, happy with his surprise. She knew he believed he was making everything right. It would be easy to let her plans go, to smile and thank him. After all, the letter was more important. If Mam'selle made the dress, there would be more time to work on the letter.

But then she heard Grandma as if she stood in the doorway. Grandma would not be smiling. She would say, *This is your assignment, Electra. You will complete it from the beginning.*

Grandma would be right. The dress *was* her assignment. To let Mam'selle sew the dress would feel as wrong as taking the doll from Miss Tompkins's room in the first place.

But what of Grandpa? If she turned down his surprise, the sparkle would leave his eyes. The pleased look would fade.

He would never answer questions about that mysterious letter.

"Now for the bow," the seamstress said, turning to rolls of ribbon.

"Mam'selle." Lexie steeled herself. She didn't like feeling ungrateful to the seamstress and to Grandpa. It would be easier to leave the dress to an expert. It would be made the right way. She wouldn't be embarrassed by her own effort. It would get done. Why shouldn't she say yes?

Easy would be wrong. She didn't need to hear Grandma say the words. In her heart, she knew what she had to do. "Mam'selle, I have to make the dress myself. It's . . . expected."

Mam'selle exchanged a glance with Grandpa. "I believe your grandmama helped you before."

Lexie thought of Miss Tompkins saying, "Your grandmother may help you." But Mam'selle would do more than help. She wanted the dress to be perfect, a dress she could display in her window to show her skill. Lexie wouldn't have any part in making that dress.

If Mam'selle Maxine makes the dress, I'll be disappointed, Lexie realized, and before she could change her mind, she said, "*Help* is allowed, but I have to make it myself."

To her surprise, Mam'selle's smile dimpled again. "Grandpapa can be proud. You are young for such strong character."

Grandpa got to his feet. Lexie waited for him to say he wasn't proud at all, that she had refused his special surprise. But he put his arm around her shoulders and squeezed gently. "I wasn't thinking, honey. The dress should be yours to make. But you can let Mam'selle advise you."

The stiffness vanished from Lexie's shoulders. She smiled up at Grandpa as Mam'selle Maxine clasped her hands together. "*Bon!* Good! We will begin with the fabric. This striped pattern, yes?"

Doubt rushed back. How could she accept expensive fabric Mam'selle Maxine could sell to a customer? It might have been worthwhile to

Mam'selle for a dress to display in her window. She could probably sew it together in a day. Lexie knew it would take her the entire week to finish.

She felt like she was closing a door on Emily Grace, but she shook her head. "It wouldn't be right."

"The stripes are not right? Then perhaps this one with flowers?"

"No," Lexie said, trying not to look at the beautiful fabric. "I mean, I can't take your nice material. I . . . I'll find something."

As Grandpa squeezed her shoulder again, Mam'selle laughed, reminding Lexie of the musical bells over the doorway. "This one will go far in life," she said to Grandpa. "You must tell me how she does." Then her smile widened. "But I have the inspiration! A doll does not require great lengths of fabric. You will pick through my scrap bin. Among the cut bits and roll ends, you are sure to find enough material!"

When the modiste pulled out a basket brimming with pieces of cut fabric, the colors and textures looked like a treasure trove. Lexie could hardly believe that her problems were unraveling as fast as the stitches in her knit scarf.

But thinking of the scarf made her think of

Grandma, and the bright feeling faded. Grandma would say that she had to make the dress all by herself as a punishment for taking the doll from Miss Tompkins's room. Maybe she could keep Grandma from knowing about Mam'selle Maxine's help? She might even be allowed to sew the dress here in the shop.

No. Keeping things from Grandma had gotten her into trouble in the first place. And that lie, even though it was an accident, had hurt Grandma and her. "Whatever happens," she whispered to herself as she picked through the fabric scraps, "this time I'm going to tell Grandma everything."

While Grandpa returned to the bank, Lexie all but danced down the street, clutching her bundle of fabric. In Mam'selle's scrap basket, she had found a sizable piece of the same violet-striped cloth so perfect for Emily Grace. She was sure there was enough for a doll dress.

Her luck held. Grandma stood next door, talking to a neighbor who was sweeping her walk and didn't notice Lexie with her bundle.

Lexie hurried into the house. She would start on the new dress before Grandma could learn about it and think up a reason to object.

Scissors, she told herself. They were in the sewing-machine cabinet.

She ran into the kitchen, then glanced toward the front door. Grandma was still outside. She pulled open the top drawer of the cabinet. The scissors were there, but her fingers wouldn't let go of the drawer to reach for them. An envelope lay across the scissors, a familiar envelope.

In her mind, everything else fell away. All she could see was her mother's handwriting.

This was the letter Grandma had shoved into her apron pocket on Friday. She must have put it here later, when she put the apron into the laundry hamper. She would think a drawer of the sewing-machine cabinet was the last place Lexie would look after seeing her doll's dress burned in the kitchen stove.

"I'd better open it before Grandma comes back." Lexie reached for the letter. Her breath ached through her chest. "Mama wrote something about me," she said softly. "She asked me to come to San Francisco."

Wasn't that what Grandma had been saying, that they couldn't afford a steamship ticket?

Lexie had to know. Her fingers trembled as she lifted the envelope flap. It was wrong to read a letter meant for someone else. "But it's about me," she whispered. "I know it is. Doesn't that make it right? Why shouldn't I read a letter about me?"

She heard Grandma on the front porch, calling good-bye to the neighbor. Shoving the letter under the bundle of fabric, Lexie darted for the stairs. As she reached the first step, Grandma came into the hall.

CHAPTER 16

The letter and the violet-striped cloth felt enormous in Lexie's hands. She could not have been more aware of them if she had held Emily Grace, tilting and crying out, "Mama!"

She didn't know how to tell Grandma about the fabric. There was no way to explain the letter.

"Here you are!" Grandma said. "Did you and Grandpa enjoy your ice cream?"

Lexie felt her heart beating against her chest like a trapped bird. Sometimes the only way out was straight ahead. She plunged into the truth. "Grandpa took me to see the dressmaker, Miss Maxine. I mean, Mam'selle."

"Oh?" Grandma's smile said she was amused by the dressmaker's pretense at being French, but her eyes held hard questions. "Is she going to make the new dress for you?"

"No!" Lexie clutched the fabric bundle closer. "She let me dig through her scrap bin for material. And she showed me pictures in her book."

"Hmm." Grandma slipped her shawl from her shoulders and hung it on the coat tree beside the front door.

"I told her I had to make it myself," Lexie added.

Grandma nodded. "Did you find scraps you could use?"

Lexie glanced down at the bundle. "Yes. Some of the pieces came from ends of her rolls of cloth. They were too small to make dresses for ladies. I'm sure there's enough for a doll."

"Good." This time, Grandma's smile held approval. "I'm glad to see you are resourceful. You had best get started. I'll be up to see if you need help laying out the pattern before you make the first cuts."

The letter loomed in Lexie's mind. When Grandma thought about the scissors, she would remember that letter. Courage fled. Turning, Lexie rushed up the stairs to her room.

She shoved the letter under her pillow. She longed to read it but felt guilty for taking it. Would Grandma think that was as bad as taking the doll? *Maybe I can pretend I haven't seen the letter at all.* Grandma would know that wasn't true.

Questions led to more questions, and none of them had answers. Lexie put the whole swirling problem from her mind and carefully smoothed the violet-striped cloth on her bed. "Look, Annie. Won't this make a pretty dress for Emily Grace?"

She thought her old doll looked sad and added quickly, "There may be enough for you, too."

The awfulness of burning the first dress rushed back. She made herself think instead of making a new pattern from a newspaper she would take from the trash. She needed to make the pattern while she still remembered the size for each piece.

But that pattern was for the first dress, the one that burned. Would the pattern pieces she remembered work for the dress in the picture Mam'selle Maxine had shown her?

The door opened and Grandma stepped inside. "Those are the scraps? My goodness, Maxine wastes a good bit of her material to be throwing away all of that. Well, I suppose her prices are high enough to cover her cost."

Lexie wondered if she should speak up for Mam'selle, who had been kind. As she hesitated, Grandma looked toward the bed. Her eyes narrowed. "What is that?"

"What?" Lexie got off the bed, feeling as if she were made of wood. The letter must be showing under the pillow. Why hadn't she been more careful?

Maybe she wouldn't have to ask to go to Mama in San Francisco. Maybe Grandma would send her there to be rid of her. That should have been a happy thought. Somehow, it wasn't, not if Grandma sent her away in anger.

But Grandma lifted the side of the mattress and pulled out the ruined pink knit scarf. Lexie had almost forgotten it was there.

"I tried to make a dress for Emily Grace," she said, talking fast. "I thought it could go over her head and have a belt, but when I cut it, all the stitches started unraveling and I couldn't make them stop."

"Oh, my goodness." Grandma held up the scarf. Light showed through the ladder-like strips where the stitches had unknitted. She seemed to be fighting a smile. How could she think the ruined scarf was funny?

As Lexie stared at the scarf, Grandma patted her shoulder. "Some lessons have to be learned the hard way. I expect this scarf taught you a good deal about knitted fabric."

"Yes," Lexie said on a rush of breath.

Grandma looked thoughtful, tilting her head as she turned the scarf one way, then another. "I don't believe this is entirely a lost cause."

"It isn't?" Lexie hardly dared believe the gentleness in Grandma's voice.

"The stitches ran from the cut in the center, but the sides are still intact. Suppose we use the machine to sew a tight line a few inches from each end," Grandma said. "And we'll sew along the sides of the part that hasn't unraveled. Then we'll cut off the rest and let the edges fringe. The pink should make a pretty scarf for that violet-striped material when it's made into a dress."

Lexie felt as though Miss Tompkins had decided to cancel a math test on a day when Lexie wasn't ready for it. "That will work." She glanced at her old soft doll. "Do you think Annie could have one, too?"

Grandma's smile warmed her whole face. "There will be plenty left to make a scarf for Annie."

Lexie could almost relax, but she knew this

moment was fragile. As soon as Grandma thought about scissors, she was going to remember that letter. And the scissors were lying right there on the bed with the fabric.

She drew in a breath for courage. "Grandma, there's something else. When I got the scissors . . . I found Mama's letter. I didn't read it, though."

That probably wouldn't mean much to Grandma. They both knew she had meant to read the letter, even though it wasn't addressed to her.

Grandma's brows lifted. Lexie braced for a scolding. To her surprise, Grandma sighed and said instead, "You may read it. Your grandfather and I had doubts because we didn't want to get your hopes up. Your mother sometimes sees things as she wants them to be, not the way they really are."

Lexie wasn't sure what that meant and didn't care. Grandma wasn't angry. That single thought warmed her like a hug as she reached for the letter. Mama's handwriting, even her scent, were so vivid that just holding the envelope brought her into the room as if she were standing there.

Longing clung so tightly for a moment, Lexie couldn't think. She blinked hard to clear misty eyes, then slipped out the single page.

CHAPTER 17

*C*alifornia greetings, *Mother and Father Lewis,* the letter read in Mama's breezy voice, as if she stood beside Lexie saying her words aloud.

I know you're having a swell time with Lexie, but here's nifty news! Lexie must have told you I'll be warbling good-bye to the dolls when they leave for Japan. Now the program people have come up with a keen idea!

They think it would be a hoot for one of the girls who helped collect pennies to buy and dress the dolls to sing the good-bye song with me. Ain't that the cat's pajamas? So if you'll put Lexie on a steamer to San Francisco, we'll sing the dolls off to Japan together!

"As you see," Grandma said, her voice sounding far away to Lexie, "your mother has suggested you join her."

Happiness soared through Lexie. To sing with Mama! To be with her again!

"In my day," Grandma said, "proper young ladies did not perform in public."

"But I have already," Lexie protested. "There's a restaurant in our building—I mean where we used to live. Mama and I sang together for people there. They liked us!"

"Humph." Grandma shook her head. "Leaving aside whether your singing in public would be proper, there's the matter of the cost. Your grandfather and I would never allow you to travel alone. It would not be safe. And steamship tickets are expensive."

Grandma's forehead creased the way it did when she worked over the household accounts. "The price for two passages to San Francisco and back . . ."

"I'll help. I have two dimes and a nickel saved up from my birthday."

Grandma shook her head. "Maybe in another

year we can make the trip. We could plan for a spring month, when the weather would be nice."

"The dolls are leaving this year," Lexie said. "On January seventh!"

"You'll join the party to say good-bye to Emily Grace and the others leaving from Portland. I can hear my mother now saying that will be celebration enough for a young girl."

Lexie wanted to say, *Girls in your day didn't get to have much fun, did they?* But Grandma would only call her mouthy. So she kept the thought to herself.

It wasn't fair for old-fashioned ideas to spoil things. "The ship is carrying more than dolls, Grandma. It's carrying friendship. And hope. Miss Tompkins says the dolls might keep a war from starting! That's important!"

"What's important to an eleven-year-old girl is to grow up safely with a good reputation," Grandma said. "Because Grandpa and I love you, our job is to see that that happens."

Arguments rushed into Lexie's head. She opened her mouth, then closed it. Arguing would just set Grandma's mind harder.

The thought of walking all the way to San

Francisco was no good. Another look at the map in the classroom had told her that. Even if she could walk all the way, a lot of it over mountains, she wouldn't get there in time.

But she could be as stubborn as Grandma. *The cost won't be as high as Grandma thinks,* she promised herself. *I won't need tickets both ways. Once I get to San Francisco, I'm not coming back.*

She wondered why she felt a quiver at that. It wouldn't be the first time she had left friends and gone to a new school. But this time, she would be leaving Grandma and Grandpa. And that made tears well up, so she swallowed hard and reached for the dress pattern, hoping Grandma wouldn't see them.

"You've shown admirable resilience, Electra," Grandma said, sounding warmer. "A lot of folks, even grown folks, would lose heart at the first setback. You've mustered strength and kept on. You can be proud of that." She cleared her throat. "I don't mind saying you've made me proud."

The praise surprised Lexie and meant a lot, because Grandma didn't offer praise lightly. She believed that too much praise spoiled a child. Lexie had heard her say that to Grandpa.

I'm not giving up, she promised herself. *I'll ask*

again later. As some of the weight left her shoulders, she said, "I'll ask Mam'selle about changing the pattern to be like the dress she showed me."

She heard her mistake almost before the words left her lips. Grandma's brows shot up. She looked as insulted as if Lexie had suggested asking a neighbor for ways to flavor her soup.

"You sketch out that dress you like," Grandma said. "Between us, we'll make do."

Grandma was starting to understand how important this was. Lexie smiled her thanks. When she heard Lexie had written the best letter, wouldn't even Grandma see that she deserved to sail down to San Francisco with Emily Grace and the other dolls?

A few days later, Lexie cornered Jack while he was stacking firewood behind the house. "Are you still mad?"

He dropped a log on the stack. "I suppose we're even."

"I'm glad. Because I need to read my letter for the doll to you. You have good ideas. I like the one about putting in a Japanese poem."

He looked pleased. Telling him he had a good idea must have made him happy. She rushed on before he could change his mind. "I wrote a new one, one that doesn't make me sad. Do you want to hear it?"

He shrugged. "Go ahead."

She brought her haiku to mind:

"My doll travels far,
Her arms open wide for hugs.
Will blossoms greet her?"

"Sounds good." Jack turned back to the firewood. "You're turning into a regular Japanese poet."

Lexie pushed his shoulder in a way that meant she liked hearing that but didn't believe it. New hope for winning the contest sizzled through her.

For the rest of that week, Lexie spent every spare minute on the dress and the letter. Every time she reread her words, she changed one or two, then the next time changed them back. Finally, on Sunday evening, she decided the letter was ready. It had to be. And the dress was finished, too.

When she gave the new dress to Miss Tompkins Monday morning, the teacher held it up for everyone to see. "You've done a fine job, Electra. This dress can certainly travel to Japan with Emily Grace."

"You didn't make that," Louise said from two rows over. "Your grandma did."

The glow from the teacher's words vanished like a popped bubble. Lexie felt everyone turning to look at her. Louise had used her superior voice, the one that said, *Stay in the shade. The sunlight belongs to me.*

"Grandma told me how," Lexie shot back. "I sewed every single stitch myself!"

Louise's mouth curved in a half smile that said as clearly as words that Lexie must be lying.

"She made it," Jack said, surprising her. "I saw her working on it myself. And she did a good job."

"Oh, Ja-ack," Ollie taunted.

Jack looked down, color splotching his cheeks. Lexie smiled her thanks, but he wouldn't look at her. She wondered when he'd seen her working on the dress. Had he come by to end their argument and decided not to interrupt when he saw her sewing with Grandma?

Miss Tompkins called attention to a sentence diagram on the blackboard. Lexie had trouble thinking about adjectives and nouns. Despite Jack's defense, she kept hearing Louise's accusation and seeing others glance toward her with doubt in their eyes.

Feeling that Jack was the only one who believed in her, whether he wanted to talk to her or not, Lexie started toward him at noon recess. One of Louise's friends stopped her. "You're a liar. Louise said you didn't make that dress."

"I did too!"

"She made it," Jack said, coming over. "Go chase spiders, Alma."

"Where is Louise?" Lexie asked as Alma kicked dirt toward Jack. "I want to talk to her."

Alma tossed her head, ignoring Jack as he kicked the dirt in her direction. "I think she went around back to look for woodpeckers."

"Better not tell her ma," Jack said. "Mrs. Wilkins says the only birds a lady cares about are the ones she wears on her hats."

As Alma flounced away, Lexie called, "Tell Louise I'm looking for her."

"Forget her," Jack said. "Nobody listens to Louise. Nobody who counts."

"Thanks."

He shrugged and walked away, then turned.

"This is the big day, remember? They're going to collect the letters. That's all that matters."

Trouble with Louise vanished in a rush. Jack was still her friend, and the day she'd been waiting for was here at last.

Moments later, the class bell rang. As Lexie followed the others inside, all she could think of was the letter. The classroom faded while her mind filled with images of Mama and San Francisco and a big ship at the dock and of herself standing on the pier with Mama, singing good-bye to the dolls.

CHAPTER 18

The others settling into their seats might have been in a separate classroom. For Lexie, the whispers and scrapes of chairs faded. She could think only of the letter. Who would judge? How soon? Would each of them read their letters aloud or just turn them in to be judged?

The letter in her desk was as perfect as she could make it. Or was it? Should she take it out and read it again to be sure?

No, there was no time left. And the letter said exactly what it should, exactly what she wanted. She would leave it in the desk until it was time to hand it in so she wouldn't be tempted to mess it up with erasures that she would only change and change again.

Instead, she stared at the map with the gold stars over three cities and waited.

The minutes passed slowly, but at last, the classroom door opened. Mr. Wilkins came in with a cardboard box. He meant to collect them, then.

For an awful moment, Lexie panicked. What if Louise's father threw out the letters and kept just the one written by his daughter? She squeezed her hands together to keep them from shaking. Mr. Wilkins put a lot of store by honor. That's what Grandpa said. Her letter would be given a fair chance, along with all the others.

Miss Tompkins welcomed their visitor. Turning to the class, she introduced him, as if everyone in the class didn't already know that Louise's father was the head of the school board.

Mr. Wilkins was tall and wore a dress suit as crisp as their principal's. He looked over the class, not taking any special notice of Louise. Louise didn't try to draw his attention. She sat model-student straight, with her hands on her desk and her expression serious. Maybe life wasn't as easy for her as Lexie had thought from looking at her expensive clothes and beauty shop haircuts.

"I understand the boys were not interested in this project." Mr. Wilkins swept a severe glance over the boys. Even Ollie showed good sense for once and remained silent. "Therefore, it gives me pleasure to announce a prize the school board will award to the girl who has written the best letter." Mr. Wilkins sounded as serious as Louise looked. Lexie could scarcely draw a breath. Were the rumors true? Would the winner go to San Francisco?

"You have all contributed your efforts and your pennies to purchase and clothe this doll." He placed one hand on Emily Grace's head. "You know this doll will join thousands of others on a journey to the country of Japan. Many are already aboard trains traveling across America toward the port of San Francisco. Who can tell me why?"

He pointed to a girl in the first row. She answered promptly. "They're for children who live in all parts of Japan."

"Yes." He motioned to Alma. "But why are we sending dolls to those children? Can you tell us?"

"For peace," Alma said. "We hope the dolls will carry our message of friendship."

Lexie knew all that. Everyone did. They had talked about it for weeks and weeks. Why didn't

Mr. Wilkins get to the contest and the mystery prize?

"Dolls from our neighbors will join this doll of yours here in Portland," Mr. Wilkins said. "A small celebration will be held on the dock beside the Willamette River. We will all wish them a safe journey to San Francisco. With dolls from all over America, they will board a ship and travel across the Pacific Ocean to Japan."

Lexie shifted in her seat. Others were becoming restless, too. Miss Tompkins's expression warned them to be patient.

Mr. Wilkins placed his box on the teacher's desk. "We are planning a farewell ceremony near the wharf here. No doubt it will pale before the grand celebration to be held in San Francisco."

He looked around the room again. *"If only I could be there.* Isn't that what each of you is thinking?" A faint smile made his thin mustache rise. "But perhaps you have heard an exciting rumor. I am pleased to confirm that rumor. One of you *will* take part in the dolls' farewell from that California city."

Mr. Wilkins went on to say that the winner would be named during the send-off party for the dolls planned for the Portland wharf in January. Lexie's heart pounded so hard she could hear it. Jack could probably hear it from his desk across the aisle.

The girls who had written letters were called to the front of the room, one row at a time, to put their entries into Mr. Wilkins's box.

Lexie's turn was coming up. She reached into her desk for her letter, then frowned. Where was the sheet of paper that should have been on top of her books? She slid her hand over, then under the books. Nothing.

She slipped from her desk and knelt on the floor to peer into the opening. Books. Her pencil. An eraser.

"What are you doing?" Jack asked in a whisper.

"My letter. It's not here."

"Look again."

She yanked the books onto the seat.

"Electra," Miss Tompkins warned, "bring your letter to Mr. Wilkins or sit down."

"I can't find my letter! It isn't here!"

Lexie opened one book after another, shaking them. Nothing fell out. "It's gone! My letter! It's gone!"

"I am sorry to hear that," Miss Tompkins said,

sounding as if she really was sorry. "You may have forgotten to bring it with you this morning."

"No!" Lexie felt inside the desk as if her fingers could find the paper her eyes couldn't see. Inside, she felt as if she had swallowed an ice-cream sundae all at once. "It was here! Now it's gone!"

"You probably dropped it on your way to school." Disapproval made Mr. Wilkins's voice hard. She didn't care what he thought. Where was her letter? It *had* to be here.

She was sure she had put it in her desk before class. She took it out and put it back every day. She took it home with her every night to work on it over and over. What if Miss Tompkins was right? What if the letter was still in her bedroom?

The sick feeling spread up her throat as girls from across the room finished placing their entries in the box. Mr. Wilkins closed the lid.

"Wait!" Lexie grabbed her pencil. "I remember every word. I'll write it again."

Mr. Wilkins glanced at the clock on the back wall. "The contest is over, young lady." He picked up the box. "Good luck to all of you." He might as well have said *all the rest of you!* After a nod to Miss Tompkins, he strode to the door.

"But I can write it again. It will just take a minute!" In her mind, Lexie saw Mama on the dock, her brown hair bobbed short and shifting against her cheeks as she turned her head, looking for her daughter.

"Please wait," she called after Mr. Wilkins. "Please!"

CHAPTER 19

As Mr. Wilkins carried the box of letters into the hall and closed the door behind him, Lexie lurched to her feet. She clamped one hand over her mouth. "Miss Tompkins, I think I'm going to throw up!" She turned and ran for the door.

Behind her, she heard Miss Tompkins say in a worried voice, "Jack, go after her. If she feels up to walking home, please see that she reaches her grandparents safely."

Once in the hallway, Lexie gulped for air. Her stomach began to settle. She braced one hand on the wall.

Mr. Wilkins stood in the doorway of the princi-pal's office at the front of the school. Lexie watched him, sickness forgotten. He still had the box of letters.

Where would he take them? Would he leave them in the office until it was time for the judges to read them? Could she write her letter again and slip it into the box when no one was looking?

Jack came up beside her. "You look like puke."

Maybe Jack would help her get a new entry into the box. She turned to ask him, but down the hall, Mr. Wilkins called good day to the office staff. She spun around as he walked out the front door, still carrying the box.

"Oh, no!" She ran to the door. When she pushed it open, she saw Mr. Wilkins place the box on the backseat of his Packard, then climb behind the wheel.

She ran down the stairs, but she was far too late. Mr. Wilkins drove away. His automobile backfired. She felt the blast all through her body. Her feet kept running, carrying the rest of her with them. When she reached the gatepost outside her grandparents' house, she stopped and gasped for breath.

"You want me to get your grandma?" Jack asked, coming up beside her.

"No. Go back to school. I'll be all right." She leaned her cheek against the flat top of the gatepost.

Jack hesitated, but after a moment, she heard him turn and walk away. Hot tears rolled down her cheeks and onto the gatepost.

Much later, she heard the front door. Grandma hurried to her. "Good heavens, child. What has happened to you?"

She felt Grandma's arm around her, warm and caring, as she led her into the house.

It was a long time before she could tell Grandma about the missing letter. She sat at the kitchen table with a glass of milk Grandma had warmed on the stove. "I don't care who wins! It doesn't matter now. And I won't go to that good-bye party."

"Of course you will go." Grandma sat across from her. Her eyes were kind, but her mouth took on the stubborn look Lexie knew all too well. "You are a Lewis, with steel in your spine. You will go to that party, and you will congratulate the girl who wins."

"I can't." But even as she said the words, she felt strength coming back, and with it a mind-set as hard as Grandma's. If she stayed away, everyone would know why. She didn't want them laughing or, worse, pitying her. Grandma was right. "I'll go."

"Of course you will." Grandma patted her shoulder before getting to her feet. "Wash your hands and face, then come help me fix dinner. The best medicine for disappointment is hard work."

Lexie didn't know if that was true, but she felt a little better until she ran upstairs and searched all through her room for the letter that wasn't there.

On the day of the good-bye party for the dolls, Grandpa had to work. Jack's mother couldn't leave the boardinghouse, so Jack, Lexie, and Grandma climbed aboard a crowded trolley to ride through a light rain to the Portland wharf.

Jack held on to an overhead strap near Lexie and looked at her as if afraid she might break down. "You okay?"

"Of course." She made herself smile. "This is going to be the bee's knees. I can't wait to congratulate the winner!"

Even though she had used one of Mama's flapper expressions, she felt Grandma's approval. A glance at Jack said he didn't believe her, flapper expression or not.

The Oregon Journal had published a story about the dolls and the farewell celebration. The public was invited, so the school had arranged to use a large warehouse along the dock.

Folding chairs filled the room. Already parents

and children were finding seats. Occasional shafts of sunlight broke through the high windows, glimmering over clothing and striping the wood floor. A Christmas tree stood below the stage at one end, but the rest of the room decorations were meant to make the audience think of Japan.

Several dolls sent from other towns and nearby states stood in their upright boxes along a table at the head of the room. Each one had a small suitcase at her feet. The dolls' tickets and passports lay nearby. They would all leave from here for San Francisco.

The children and their families and friends filed by the tables for a closer look at the dolls. Grandma opened the passport beside Emily Grace. Inside, it gave her name and said she was a good citizen, promising, "She will obey all the laws and customs of your country."

Grandma marveled. "It's as though she were going traveling."

"She is," Lexie reminded her.

"You're right. She's going farther than either of us is likely to go."

Lexie looked sadly at Emily Grace. She stood near the center of the line of dolls, smiling out at the audience as if she knew adventure lay just ahead and couldn't wait to begin. "I'll miss you," Lexie whispered.

A ship's horn blasted outside on the river, briefly overwhelming conversation in the warehouse as everyone settled into seats.

"You okay?" Jack asked again, dropping into a folding chair beside Lexie. She nodded, giving him the big smile she had practiced. No one was going to watch her heart break.

"You look like the Cheshire Cat," he said. When she made her smile even bigger, he laughed and turned to talk to a friend in the row behind. At least he was sitting beside her. She had half expected him to find a seat across the room.

The high-school band tuned their instruments at one side of the dolls' table. Excitement crackled as everyone waited to hear who, of all the girls in the class, would be going to San Francisco with Emily Grace.

Lexie looked at the other dolls. Many were from schools or towns in Oregon. Others were from the nearby states of Washington and Idaho. She knew that many groups from churches to parent-teacher organizations and Girl Scouts had helped buy and dress the dolls.

"Look there," Grandma said. "That one's

dressed up like one of Florence Nightingale's nurses. Weren't they supposed to look like average American girls?"

"That's what the instructions said." Lexie was surprised by the clothing choices, too. Another was a boy doll dressed in a police uniform. What would the people at the girls' festival in Japan think of that?

Jack elbowed her in the side. She glanced at him, then to the head of the room. Mr. Wilkins had just walked to the front. He stood beside the dolls and waited for the audience to grow silent.

Jack leaned closer to whisper, "He'll have a lot to say and all of it boring."

Lexie giggled, then put a hand over her mouth when Grandma gave her a warning look.

Jack was right. Mr. Wilkins did talk too long before the band played and again when they finished. She stopped listening and instead mentally listed things she could have been doing instead of sitting here pretending to be happy for someone else.

1. *Sleeping.*
2. *Nestling into Grandpa's rocking chair with a book.*
3. *Playing with Annie.*

4. Writing to Mama. But what would she say,
that she'd lost their one chance to be together?

She forced a smile to her lips. She was going to congratulate the winner, whoever it was.

Jack leaned closer, his thoughts apparently following hers. "Did you find that letter?"

"No." Since she'd met him, Jack had played a lot of tricks. Could Jack have taken the letter? Could that be his idea of a joke?

She pushed the thought away. Even Jack wouldn't make a joke of a letter he knew meant everything to her.

At the front of the room, Mr. Wilkins was finally running out of words, or at least turning to new ones. "The dolls will not leave until January fourth," he said. "We are celebrating today, before the Christmas break, so our winner will not be left in suspense." When he introduced Mrs. Phipps, a parent volunteer who was in charge of the letter-writing contest, Lexie felt her heart leap. Despite herself, she leaned forward to hear who had won.

Mrs. Phipps smiled at Louise's father. "Mr. Wilkins's generosity has made it possible for our sixth-grade class to send a doll to Japan for the girls' festival of Hinamatsuri. We are grateful to him."

After applause, she turned to the audience. "All those who entered the contest put their thoughts and hearts into their letters," she said. "However, the exceptional work of one stood apart from all the others. It was a clear winner from the beginning."

Fresh pain gripped Lexie. *No one put their heart into their letter more than I did.* But no one would hear the letter she had lost.

To her surprise, Grandma clasped one hand over hers. The warm touch helped her relax a little.

"Since none of the boys were interested," Mrs. Phipps continued, "it gives me great pleasure to announce the name of the young lady who will receive a paid trip for herself and her chaperone. The two of them will accompany all these fine dolls to San Francisco, California."

Despite Grandma's comforting touch, Lexie sank lower in her chair. Excitement swept through the crowd. It made her feel the loss of her letter even more. The paper must have slipped from her book while she walked to school, but she had looked and looked for it. Her eyes blurred, but she would not cry. She would smile and congratulate the winner. Somehow.

Mrs. Phipps unfolded a paper. "The young lady who impressed us with her letter and will be traveling with the dolls to San Francisco is"—she paused, glancing over the crowd with a smile while an expectant hush hung over everyone—"Miss Louise Wilkins."

Lexie's breath caught sharply. *Louise.* Of course it was Louise. Hadn't she always known it would be?

She felt Grandma look at her, probably wondering if she would remember to smile and congratulate the winner. She couldn't think of a single thing she would rather do less.

Beside her, Jack said with surprising loyalty, "She brought in the most money. Maybe that's why they chose her."

In silence, not trusting her voice, Lexie watched Louise thread her way from the audience and walk to the front of the room. She looked proud and not at all surprised.

"Congratulations, Louise," Mrs. Phipps said. "Your letter is lovely. We would like to have you read it to everyone."

Louise looked startled. She took the paper Mrs. Phipps was handing her and looked over at her father, then out at the audience. Her gaze brushed Lexie before moving away.

There was a long pause. Mrs. Phipps said, "Go ahead, dear."

Louise looked at the paper again, then said with defiance in her voice, "This is what I wrote." When she began to read, her voice rang over the crowd.

Jack nudged Lexie. "Her letter sounds a lot like yours."

It did, but they must have all written the same things about hoping the girls in Japan would welcome Emily Grace and telling them the doll brought their friendship with her.

"I decided to include a Japanese poem to say how I felt," Louise finished. "It's called a haiku, and this is what it says:

"My doll travels far,
Her arms open wide for hugs.
Will blossoms greet her?"

Lexie felt as if she'd been punched in the stomach. While the audience murmured appreciation, she sat in stunned silence. "Grandma," she said, her voice sounding strangled.

Jack shot to his feet. "You didn't write that poem! Lexie did! You're the one who stole the letter from her desk!"

CHAPTER 20

J ack Harmon!" While Lexie looked at him in astonishment, Mrs. Wilkins rose from her chair. Her face flushed such a bright pink that the feathered dove on her cloche looked in danger of bursting into flame. "How dare you spoil Louise's proud moment?"

"She shouldn't be proud," Jack said, setting his chin at a stubborn angle. "She didn't write that."

"I did too write it." Louise darted a glance between her mother and Jack.

Who did Grandma believe? Remembering the night she had had to burn the doll dress, Lexie lurched to her feet. This time, she meant to stand up for herself. "Jack's right. I wrote that haiku." She pointed at Louise. "You took my letter from my desk."

"When could I have done that?" Louise asked in a smug voice that reminded everyone that her parents were important.

"At noon recess," Lexie shot back. "I looked for you. You weren't on the playground. Alma said you were looking for woodpeckers." And Jack said the only woodpeckers Louise's mama cared about were on her hat, but she had better not say that.

"Wicked stories," Mrs. Wilkins exclaimed. "The idea!"

"It's not a story!" Lexie rushed on. "You weren't anywhere on the playground, Louise. You were in the classroom stealing my letter!"

Mrs. Wilkins turned toward Lexie like thunder rolling in. "Young lady, you should be ashamed of yourself. We all know you have proven to be less than truthful."

Like everyone else in the audience, Grandma had been turning from one speaker to another. Now she surged to her feet. "Eleanor Wilkins, you are the one who should be ashamed. To attack a child!"

That sounded like Grandma was on her side,

Lexie thought with a rush of hope. Grandma didn't like Mrs. Wilkins, so that might have been part of it. *But she sounds angry* for *me, not* at *me.* Despite the tension in the room, she felt a corner of her heart dare to grow warmer.

"Ladies, please!" Mrs. Phipps held out her hands as if to separate the two women. "Please. We hope to *prevent* a war with these dolls, not *start* one!"

The audience laughed uneasily. Mr. Wilkins stepped forward. "Well said, Mrs. Phipps. If the two girls and the ladies will join me in private, we will get to the bottom of this."

He turned to the rest of the parents and children. "In the meantime, the first-grade class will entertain with a song popular in Japan called 'The Blue-Eyed Doll.' Here is Esther Hall to tell you the story behind the song."

Six-year-old Esther marched importantly to the front of the room, dressed in a kimono. The rest of the first-grade class lined up behind her, twirling paper parasols painted with butterflies and flowers. A flashlamp blazed. A reporter from the newspaper must have been there.

Grandma marched through the crowd toward

the door where Mr. Wilkins waited, towing Lexie with her. Onstage, little Esther began, "The song is about a celluloid doll that came on a ship."

Jack made his way through the audience, following them to the smaller room. Lexie gave him a quick, grateful smile. The moment the door closed behind her, Mrs. Wilkins said to Grandma, "I hope you are not forgetting a certain lie over the matter of the doll's dress."

Grandma's mouth took a dangerous set.

Mr. Wilkins motioned to chairs around a long table. "Please, everyone. Sit down."

Lexie sank into a chair beside Grandma, feeling excited and scared and angry all at the same time. Was there a chance she might be declared the winner after all? The winning letter was hers, even if it did have Louise's name on it.

She wasn't the one lying. She hadn't lied about the dress, either. She just hadn't found a good time to tell the truth. But she should have. Would all this be different if she had been truthful with Grandma from the start? Could *when* you told the truth be as important as *how* you told it?

"Louise," said Mr. Wilkins, breaking into Lexie's swirling thoughts, "have you anything to say?"

Louise leaped to her feet. "I wrote the letter and the poem. If she says she did, she's lying. Again."

"You're the liar," Lexie said. She started to get up, but Grandma reached over to press her hand and she sank back down.

Mr. Wilkins said quickly, "Young lady, you will have your chance to speak."

Jack jumped to his feet. "Then I'll speak. Lexie read her letter to me days ago. We talked a lot about the poem she was putting in it. That's her letter Louise read."

"He's mad at me," Louise told her father, tears brimming in her eyes. "Because I won't kiss him. Like she does. He'll say anything for her!"

"What?" Lexie exclaimed.

Jack's cheeks blazed red. "I don't want *anybody* kissing on me!"

"Enough!" Mr. Wilkins strode to the door and held it open. "You may rejoin the others, Jack. You have had your say."

"But . . ." Jack looked at Lexie. She shrugged, wanting to sink through the floor. Fiercely, she wondered, what would Mama do? She knew the answer to that. Mama would hold her head up and laugh at someone trying to embarrass her. Lexie didn't feel much like laughing, but she raised her chin and stared straight at Louise.

Louise was too busy looking sorrowful to notice. Anger and disappointment crashed together inside Lexie, helped along by outrage. How could anybody believe Louise, with her pout and phony tears?

"Louise," her father said, returning to his seat after closing the door behind Jack, "tell us about the letter. You are the only one who included a Japanese poem. How did you think of doing that?"

"She didn't." Despite the pressure of Grandma's hand, Lexie couldn't keep silent. "I did! We all wrote haiku in class. Mine was best, and Jack Harmon said I should put it in my letter. Then I wrote a different one because the first one was sad. That's the one Louise stole!"

Louise looked at her father with fresh tears shining. "Jack did suggest putting in *my* haiku. That was when I talked to him about *my* letter. He must have told *her.* When she kissed him."

CHAPTER 21

Lexie silently promised never to kiss a boy again in her entire life. She had only done it to spite Louise. She glanced at Grandma and saw her eyes flashing. She looked like Mama when someone who should say hello remembered that she sang in clubs and looked away instead.

This was hurting Grandma, Lexie realized. She had been so upset over losing the letter, she hadn't thought about Grandma's feelings. The new warmth inside tightened into a cold lump.

"Perhaps we can solve this with a simple test." Mr. Wilkins walked again to the door, this time calling, "Mrs. Phipps, Miss Tompkins, will you join us, please?"

Miss Tompkins knows I wrote the best haiku, even if she didn't see the second one. She knows my letter disappeared. Relief swept through Lexie.

Mrs. Phipps came inside, looking as if rotting fish had been discovered under a table, causing all the guests to hold their noses. "I had such high hopes for this day," she said in a wistful tone that still managed to hold accusation. "We need to settle this quickly."

Miss Tompkins took a seat near Mr. Wilkins with a troubled look on her face. It was the same look she had had when Mr. Wilkins said there wasn't time for Lexie to rewrite her letter. But Miss Tompkins knew the truth. Didn't she?

"The girls will each write a new poem in the Japanese style," Mr. Wilkins explained. "Mrs. Phipps, we need your expertise. You read all the letters submitted for the contest. Miss Tompkins, you are familiar with the girls' work. With that understanding, we would like you both to read the two new poems and tell us which is most likely to have been written by the girl who wrote the letter."

"Oh!" Mrs. Phipps clasped her hands together. "Mr. Wilkins, I'm not sure that would be a fair test, considering the pressure they are feeling."

"Nonsense! We are not asking the girls to create art, just to prove they can write. Miss Tompkins, will you please locate pencils and two sheets of paper?"

Grandma said in a flat tone, "Electra will not have a problem."

The dove on Mrs. Wilkins's cloche fluttered as if about to fly off. "Louise will do fine."

Lexie couldn't wait to prove that Louise had stolen the letter and pretended she wrote it herself. To write haiku, you had to be calm. She tried to put everything from her mind but a new poem. Still, her thoughts jittered faster than the dove on Mrs. Wilkins's hat.

Miss Tompkins asked each girl to move to a separate end of the table. She handed out pencils and paper and told them to begin.

Lexie was sure that Louise would not write a haiku as good as the one she had. Sure, she knew how many syllables to use, but Louise had not studied the feeling a haiku should raise in the reader. Mrs. Phipps was wrong. This was going to be a fair test. It would prove who had written the letter. Lexie bent over the paper, eager to begin.

At first, she felt the others in the room watching

her, but gradually the haiku took over her mind. She counted syllables, chose words, counted again, and chose new words. The feeling had to be right.

"We'll stop now," Mr. Wilkins announced. "Those are short poems, are they not? They require only a few words. The girls have had plenty of time. Louise, stand and read your poem."

Louise stood, holding her paper in both hands.

"The dolls are leaving.
They will all sail to Japan.
We must say good-bye."

Lexie saw Mr. Wilkins nod. Didn't he know the poems usually included nature?

"Thank you, Louise," Mrs. Phipps said. "Electra, read your poem, please."

Lexie stood. The paper trembled in her hand. She drew a breath to sound more confident.

"Emily Grace glows.
Her warm smile carries friendship.
Sunlight after rain."

"Thank you," said Mr. Wilkins. "You may both take your seats. Mrs. Phipps, in your judgment, which of these girls wrote the letter?"

Mrs. Phipps looked as if she had been asked to choose among her own children. "Oh." She twisted her hands together. "Poetry is very personal. Everyone hears the words differently, depending on their own life experiences."

"I believe we have a question of style rather than one of art, which indeed can be subjective." Impatience stole into Mr. Wilkins's voice.

"Both girls have written well," Miss Tompkins said, "particularly when asked to create without warning and under considerable stress."

"But one poem must rise above the other," Mr. Wilkins warned, adding, "Mrs. Phipps, may we have your conclusion?"

Mrs. Phipps touched the tip of her tongue to her lips, which must have become dry. "They are quite similar. After all, they both address the subject of the doll leaving for Japan."

Lexie knew suddenly that Mrs. Phipps would not offend an important man who was also the head of the school board. No one was going to hear Mrs. Phipps tell Mr. Wilkins that his daughter was a liar and a thief.

Mr. Wilkins pulled out his pocket watch and gave it a meaningful look. "May we have your answer, Miss Tompkins?"

Lexie held her breath.

"As you say," Miss Tompkins said after a cautious pause, "one poem rises somewhat above the other."

Mrs. Phipps broke in. "Let us consider the handwriting." She placed the two poems on the table with the letter. "Louise shapes far rounder letters than Electra," she pointed out. "Electra's writing also shows a forward slant. Clearly, Louise's hand wrote both letter and poem."

"Thank you," Mr. Wilkins said with a smile for Louise. Lexie felt as if cold water had been thrown in her face. Of course the handwriting was the same. Louise had copied that letter.

"I have not finished," Miss Tompkins protested. "The style——"

"Yes," Mrs. Phipps said with a nervous look toward Mr. Wilkins. "The style most clearly belongs to Louise."

Miss Tompkins countered sharply. "I did not say that. Electra's poem——"

Again Mrs. Phipps broke in. "If we must discuss style, may I point out that Louise mentions travel and Japan in her poem? I believe we should declare Louise the winner."

"That was not the criteria," Miss Tompkins protested.

At the same time, Grandma exclaimed, "Give Miss Tompkins a chance to speak!"

Mrs. Wilkins stood, pushing back her chair. "We have delayed the ceremony quite long enough. Let us return to the others."

Lexie said, "But I wrote——"

Mr. Wilkins spoke over her. "Thank you, Mrs. Phipps, Miss Tompkins. The school board will wish to reward all the children for their good work. I will be making that announcement." He strode to the door. Mrs. Wilkins hurried after him, tugging Louise with her.

"That's a surprise," Grandma snapped in a tone that said the decision was no surprise to her. "Come, Electra, we are leaving."

Lexie was glad to join her and even happier to avoid congratulating Louise for stealing her letter.

Mrs. Wilkins paused in the doorway. "Really, Sophie, your attitude does your granddaughter no favor."

For a moment, Lexie thought Grandma would raise her hand to the other woman. Instead, she lifted her chin and marched out the door while Lexie hurried to follow.

Jack was waiting just outside. "Is it okay?" He

glanced from Lexie to Grandma. "I guess it didn't go too well."

He caught up with Grandma. "What if I go up on the stage? I can tell everybody Lexie read her poem to me before Louise stole it."

Grandma kept walking. "They would not believe you. The president of the *school board* has made up his mind."

"Thanks," Lexie murmured to Jack. Outside the building, she nearly walked into Grandma, who had stopped suddenly.

Overhead, gulls wheeled and quarreled. A strong smell of ships' engines along with a sharp scent of creosote from the pilings blew on a stiffening breeze. Grandma motioned toward a bench. "You two sit here. I have something to do before we catch the trolley."

Without waiting for an answer, she started down the dock.

Inside the warehouse, the first-graders were finishing "The Blue-Eyed Doll" for the second time. Their clear voices drifted through the door. Lexie listened as the blue-eyed doll in the song asked the girls of Japan to please be her friends.

A wave of sorrow washed through Lexie. She

swallowed hard, trying not to think of that celebration in San Francisco and Mama waiting for her on the wharf. "I didn't get to say good-bye to Emily Grace."

"She won't care." Jack sounded distracted.

Lexie saw that he was watching Grandma hurrying toward an office at the side of the dock, her skirt whipping in the wind from the river. Her hat lifted with every step until she reached up to hold it firmly against her head.

"Where is she going?" Lexie wondered aloud.

Jack grinned. "Maybe she's going to tell them not to sell a ticket to Louise."

"They sell tickets in there?" Lexie dropped onto the bench. The sudden hope that rushed into her mind was too big to risk giving it room in her heart. If she was wrong, disappointment would crush her.

CHAPTER 22

Grandma came back from the shipping office looking as satisfied as if she had all her Monday washing on the line before any of the neighbor women. "Come along," she said. "We don't want to miss the trolley."

"We're ahead of the crowd," Jack said, motioning toward the warehouse, where the first-graders were still singing. He looked at Lexie. "You doing all right?"

She forced herself to close her mind to the image of Emily Grace standing by her box, ready to go to Japan. "Sure. Why wouldn't I be?"

"No reason." He ran ahead to the waiting trolley.

Questions pounded through Lexie, but Grandma wasn't in an answering mood. With a sigh, Lexie found a place on the wooden seat and looked out the window, listening to the clack of the trolley wheels on the rails while it carried them from the wharf back into town.

As they walked toward their street, Grandma seemed lost in thought. Jack walked backward ahead of Lexie. "My mom's gonna have chores waiting. I gotta run."

"Okay." Lexie hesitated. "Jack, thanks. For . . . you know."

"Sure." He started away, then turned back. "Yours was the best letter. Sorry she stole it."

"Me, too." Lexie managed a smile before Jack turned again and raced toward the boardinghouse.

"He's a good friend," Grandma said, surprising Lexie. Grandma wasn't as far away in her thoughts as she'd seemed. But then she raised an eyebrow and asked, "A kissing friend?"

Lexie felt heat rush to her face. "I only kissed his cheek to make Louise mad, but that made Jack mad, and he wouldn't talk to me for days!"

Grandma smiled. "I thought it was likely something of the sort."

A question that had been burning through Lexie

burst out. "Mrs. Phipps wouldn't let Miss Tompkins talk. Why did she do that?"

Grandma shook her head. "Cecelia Phipps chose the course that was easiest for her. She will have to live with that decision. Her conscience is not our concern."

The subject was closed. Lexie could see Grandma turn a key in her mind.

It was after supper, with the dishes washed and put away, before Grandma opened that mental lock. She and Grandpa must have talked while Lexie was out back gathering an armload of firewood from the woodpile.

When Lexie came inside, Grandma was settled in a chair with mending heaped over her lap. She tucked her wooden darning egg into the toe of one of Grandpa's wool socks to hold the shape while she set to work reweaving the knit pattern across a hole. Lexie knew that when Grandma finished, Grandpa wouldn't even feel a raised bump under his toe.

Grandpa reached over to turn down the sound on the radio he'd waited in line to buy when the department store first put them on display. "Lexie, honey, we've been talking about what happened at the wharf today. Put the wood down and come over here to me."

Lexie lowered the firewood into the box beside the stove and walked over to Grandpa. A ripple of excitement shivered up her spine. He took both her hands and looked seriously into her face. "Know first of all that we love you. We want to hear in your words, from your heart, who wrote the letter Louise read today."

"I wrote it!" Shock rushed back, just as when Louise had stood up there in front of all those people and claimed the letter and poem Lexie had put her heart into for days. "I wrote every word of the letter and the haiku!"

Grandma brought the darned sock to her teeth and bit off the thread. "How did Louise lay her hands on your letter?"

"She went in at noon when nobody is supposed to be in the classroom and she copied my letter and my haiku! Word for word! She probably burned my copy in the woodstove."

"She'll pay for it, one way or another," Grandpa assured her.

Lexie could hardly hear past the anger inside. "Everyone at school is going to say I cheated! When I didn't! It was Louise!"

"You keep your head high," Grandma said. "You know who cheated."

"I always hold my head up." Lexie raised her chin even higher.

"We know you do." Grandpa gave her hands a gentle squeeze.

Grandma smiled to herself as she dropped the darning egg into another sock. She looked as if an unspoken thought had amused her, but her eyes were serious when she looked again at Lexie. "Whatever others may say, they will have to wait to say it until you come back from San Francisco."

"Come back?" Lexie looked from one to the other while hope did a crazy jig inside her. "From San Francisco?"

"You won that trip fair and square," Grandpa said. "You're going to join the dolls' big send-off and enjoy every minute of it."

"We have rainy-day money put by," Grandma assured her. "This feels like a rainy day to us. That money will be well used to send you and me on the trip."

The words danced through Lexie's head. Mama put money by for a rainy day, but she usually spent it on a new hat or sparkly ear bobs. Could it really pay for a trip to San Francisco? "When?" She was almost afraid to ask the question.

Grandma's smile was the warmest Lexie could remember seeing on her. "January fourth will be here before we know it. Run upstairs and decide what you wish to take along."

"But what about Grandpa?"

"I'll take my meals next door at the boarding-house," Grandpa assured her. "And we'll be sure to explain to Miss Tompkins why you're missing school."

Lexie hugged them both, then all but flew up the stairs. She had to think carefully what to take. Because although she and Grandma would go to San Francisco together, Grandma would be coming back here alone.

As she debated how much underwear to pack, Lexie noticed the light go on in Jack's room beyond the cherry tree. She couldn't wait to tell Jack the news. She shoved open the window and crawled out onto the branch.

A few twigs tossed at Jack's window caught his attention. He climbed into the tree beside her. The news rushed out: "I'm going to San Francisco with Emily Grace! Grandma and Grandpa used their rainy-day money for tickets."

"Great!" He slapped one hand against the tree branch. "You deserve to go. But you shouldn't have to buy a ticket. You were cheated. When you come back, we'll make Louise sorry she did that."

Lexie hesitated. "This is a secret, okay? I'm not coming back. When I get to my mama in San Francisco, I'm going to stay."

Jack whistled softly. "Your grandparents don't know?"

"Not yet. And you can't tell them. They wouldn't let me go. I know they wouldn't."

"They won't hear it from me." He leaned against the tree trunk and played with a twig, bending it back and forth until it broke. "You'd like this big tree in the summer."

"When it's shady?" Why was he changing the subject? They were talking about San Francisco.

"Not just the shade," Jack said. "There are big purple cherries on little stems all over. They're sweet as a cherry gets. It's good to sit up here and eat one right after another."

"And spit the pits," she guessed.

"Well, yeah. I'm pretty good at spitting pits where I want them to go." He grinned. "You'd probably do okay."

"Okay? I could out-spit you!" She started to

laugh, partly at the idea of competing in spitting cherry pits, but mostly out of happiness.

Jack had just given her the best gift he could have. He had given her more than a story. He had given her a reason to come back from San Francisco. Although it wouldn't work, it made her feel good that he had told her about the cherries. She almost kissed his cheek again.

But she didn't.

Grandpa brought a Christmas tree home the next morning. He set it up in the parlor while Grandma brought out a box of ornaments. Lexie put staying with Mama as far as possible from her mind. She was determined not to bring sadness to Grandma and Grandpa's Christmas.

"May I help?" she asked.

Grandpa said, "Sure, you can." But Grandma seemed to wince with every ornament Lexie put on the tree. "Not there, dear," she said at one point. "The larger balls belong on the lower branches."

Seconds later, she corrected her again. "Lexie, you have placed two red balls next to each other."

Lexie realized that each ornament had its special place and Grandma didn't much like change.

That was why she still wore her hair in a coiled braid. *But she used the rainy-day money for tickets to San Francisco. That's the kindest thing anyone has ever done for me.*

"Grandma," she said, "will you tell me where they go so I can put the ornaments where they belong?"

Grandma looked startled, then a smile came into her eyes. "Honey, you go ahead and decide where they look best. Grandpa and I might enjoy a little change this year."

As Lexie decided just where to put a silver ball with tiny beads on wires around it, Grandma's smile made her feel as warm as drinking a hot cup of cocoa. With a marshmallow on top.

When she finished, they all agreed the tree was beautiful. But to Lexie it wasn't the same as sharing a Christmas tree with Mama. She went up to her room as soon as she could without hurting Grandma and Grandpa's feelings.

Upstairs, she crawled out on the big branch of the cherry tree and twisted until she had pulled off a branch as long as her arm. She brought it inside and stood it in a milk bottle filled with a collection of beach agates. Grandpa had given her the agates, saying they once belonged to Papa. It pleased Lexie to see Papa's agates holding up her makeshift tree, as if he were there, helping her.

She colored a star on a piece of paper with a yellow crayon, then colored it again with orange to make it a darker gold, cut it out, and glued it to the top of the branch. While she was gluing strips of bright paper into loops for a chain, Jack knocked on the window. "What are you doing?"

Lexie opened the window so he could step inside. "I'm making a Christmas tree for my room."

"That's a Christmas tree?" He looked at the bare twig with a gold star glued to the top. "Most have green needles."

"You have to pretend the green." Lexie carried her chain to the tree and carefully draped it around the branches. "What's the matter, Jack? Don't you know how to pretend?"

"Sure, I do." His eyes brightened. "I'll be right back."

He scrambled through the window while Lexie started another paper chain. In minutes, he was back with a jar full of buttons. "I borrowed these from Ma. If you have some yarn, we can string them for the tree."

"Perfect." Lexie rummaged through a bag of

odds and ends Mam'selle had given her. Lace . . . rickrack . . . yarn!

Jack said, "They'll all slide together. Maybe there's not enough."

"We'll tie knots between each button."

"I'm pretty good at tying knots." He cut a length of yarn, sank onto the rug beside her, and poured out the buttons.

As they worked, Lexie told him about Christmas with Mama. It felt good to talk about her with Jack. He knew how to listen without finding fault.

"Last year was our first Christmas without Papa. We couldn't find the ornaments. We must have left them behind when we moved to a smaller place."

"That's tough," Jack said.

"Mama said even though we missed him so much sometimes it hurt to breathe, we weren't going to be Pitiful Pearls. Papa wouldn't want that. He'd want us to get on with our lives and that was what we were going to do."

"Without a Christmas tree?"

Lexie felt memories flooding in. "We had a tree. Mama draped her long ropes of pearls and rhinestones on the branches. She clipped sparkly ear bobs and brooches to the ends."

Jack whistled softly. "I'd like to have seen that."

"We laughed and sang carols and had a swell time. And it was the prettiest Christmas tree ever!" Lexie looked doubtfully at the branch in the milk bottle. "It was prettier than this one."

"Now who's forgetting to pretend?" Jack looked at the tree. "I've seen worse."

"So have I." A giggle caught Lexie by surprise. "This tree is almost as perfect as the one downstairs in the parlor."

Rain pounded the windows on Christmas morning, but right after church, Grandpa started logs blazing in the big fireplace in the parlor. They had waited to exchange gifts until after church services and a big noon meal. When Lexie felt ready to burst with impatience, Grandma said at last that it was time to open the presents.

The parlor was warm by then. Spicy gingerbread and peppermint smells drifted from a little cookie house with a candy roof Mam'selle had sent to Lexie. That and cinnamon from cider simmering on the iron range in the kitchen made the entire house smell like a big Christmas cookie.

Lexie sat on the floor pretending she was in a fairy forest that smelled of cookies and green trees.

Her name on a tag in Grandma's writing invited her to open a box wrapped in red paper. She glanced at Grandma for permission, then untied a candy cane from the ribbon on top, thanking Grandpa with a grin. The sparkle in his eyes told her that extra gift was from him. She carefully unwrapped the box, knowing that Grandma would save the paper.

Inside, she found a dictionary almost too heavy to use. "That will help with your schoolwork," Grandma said.

Lexie thanked them both, even though she wouldn't be coming back here for school and the dictionary was too heavy to take with her. Trying to ignore an ache in her heart at the thought of leaving, she gave them her gift, a silhouette profile of herself she had made in class.

They took turns holding the silhouette, turning it one way and another, admiring it. Grandpa said he would find a nice frame, and Grandma said there was a perfect spot for Lexie's picture on top of the piano.

Their praise made Lexie smile and ache inside at the same time. It was easier to be with Grandma and Grandpa than it used to be, but she was going to Mama. Nothing could make her change her mind about not coming back.

She had saved a small box from Mama for last. Big red bows all but hid the shiny gold paper. When she had them off and the box open, she lifted out a glittery headband.

She knew that headband. Last Christmas, it had circled the top of the tree, right below Mama's pretty star-shaped brooch. Lexie pressed the band to her cheek. It smelled of Mama's familiar spicy perfume and brought her close. Except for Mama herself, she couldn't have wished for a better gift.

"Mercy, child," Grandma exclaimed. "Where will you ever wear that?"

Lexie pressed Mama's headband closer. "I could wear it to school." Before Grandma could say, *What a silly idea,* she added quickly, "I guess I'd look funny. People—the others in school—they wouldn't understand."

Grandma surprised her by looking thoughtful. "It's a pretty thing, all glittery like a star." She glanced at Grandpa, then back. "What would you say to slipping it over the tree, right below the Christmas star?"

Lexie jumped up to wrap both arms around her grandma, surprising them both. "I'd like that a lot. It will be like Mama's here sharing Christmas with us!"

Grandpa pushed himself up from his big chair. "Can a grandpa get in on that hug?"

Lexie rushed to hug him, too. She couldn't see either one of them very well because her eyes were suddenly blurry.

The day of the trip to San Francisco arrived very slowly, but came at last. On an unusually sunny day for early January, Grandpa drove Lexie and Grandma to the dock. When he hugged her, Lexie held on tightly, reluctant to say good-bye. She wasn't sure when she would see him again.

Grandpa chuckled. "You have a good trip, now. Mrs. Harmon is all set up to feed me along with her boarders, so don't worry one bit."

"I wish you were coming with us," Lexie said softly.

Grandpa tousled her hair. "You just make sure to take a good long look at everything you see. I want to hear all about it when you get home."

Home . . . The word stabbed through Lexie. It was hard to leave. But in her heart, home would always be with Mama.

Mrs. Wilkins's sharp voice cut through the bright morning. "Why, look, Louise. Your little friend has come down to wish you safe journey. Show your upbringing and thank her."

Louise stuck her tongue out at Lexie and hurried toward people boarding the ship.

"Slow down, Louise!" her mother exclaimed. "Wilkins ladies do not run in public!"

Lexie murmured to Grandma, "She was just walking fast."

Mrs. Wilkins's mouth set tighter as she turned toward Grandma. "I'm sure she appreciates your coming to see her off. It's simply that she finds it difficult to forgive someone who has publicly embarrassed her."

Grandma's hand tightened on Lexie's, but her smile could have sugared oatmeal. "Lovely weather to begin a sea journey, isn't it? Come, Electra, let's find our cabin."

She walked past Mrs. Wilkins, who was surprised into silence for once. Lexie couldn't resist grinning back at her as she followed Grandma up the ramp and onto the ship.

Even while tied to the dock, the ship shifted with the river. Swells rolled beneath and slapped against the hull. Lexie bounced on her toes, enjoying the feel of the ship as they were directed to their cabin along with several other passengers.

Again, Mrs. Wilkins raised her voice. "Louise! A Wilkins lady does not gawk."

Grandma rolled her eyes. "Apparently, a Wilkins lady does screech at her daughter in public."

Giggling, Lexie followed Grandma into their cabin. As far as she was concerned, Louise deserved all the screeching she got. Inside the snug cabin, it was hard to stand still and impossible to sit quietly. The trip would take a long time, but at last she was on her way!

As soon as Grandma gave permission, Lexie raced on deck with her soft doll, Annie. She leaned against the rail, fascinated by the activity. On the ship and dock, men called orders. Planks creaked. Cables clanked against a noisy winch while they were raised into their holds.

Overhead, seagulls screeched and swooped. Lexie laughed as one snatched a fallen crumb from a visitor's breakfast roll, passing so close to the man's feet that he shouted and jumped backward.

She knew that Emily Grace and the other dolls had been packed into their boxes and then into bigger crates and stored in the hold. "I wish Emily Grace could watch all this with us," Lexie told Annie as the ship's engine rumble grew louder. Slowly, a tugboat nudged the ship into the Willamette River, headed toward the far wider Columbia. "Grandpa says it can be rough crossing the bar into the ocean," she warned Annie. "When we get there, be sure to hold on tight."

She ran along the deck toward the bow, eager for the first sight of the sea, even though she knew the ship had to travel up the Willamette while the pilot tug guided it beneath bridges. Then they would travel for hours along the Columbia before reaching the Pacific Ocean.

Willing the ship to move faster and holding Annie with one hand and the rail with the other, she made her way forward. She stopped at the sound of a girl's voice.

"You're so pretty," the girl was saying. "Your satin dress is the same blue color as your eyes."

That was Louise. Who was she talking to? Lexie moved silently around a corner of the wheelhouse. Her breath caught in her throat. Louise sat on the deck in front of the structure. She held Emily Grace in her lap.

CHAPTER 23

L exie's hand tightened on Annie. She backed around
the wheelhouse in disbelief. Louise had Emily
Grace on deck. How was that possible? All the dolls
were supposed to be in their boxes in the ship's hold.

The answer rocked her. Louise had special privileges. Again. And it wasn't fair. Lexie wanted to
rush around the corner and snatch the doll away.

Louise's voice came clearly on a twist of the
wind. "You're my only friend, Emily Grace. You
don't care if I can buy gumdrops to share or if my
papa might have a job for your papa."

Lexie didn't feel sorry for Louise, the cheat. If
she didn't have friends, it was her own fault. How
had she gotten the doll from the hold?

As if she had asked the question aloud, Louise answered, still talking to the doll. "I'm so glad I thought to ask for you after the program. Did you hear me, Emily Grace? I used my sad voice and said I needed to carry you to San Francisco. I said that would make up for the way Lexie Lewis and Jack Harmon spoiled my special day."

Fresh outrage shot through Lexie. She hadn't spoiled Louise's day. Louise had spoiled a day that should have belonged to her! No one would listen to the truth. Not Mr. Wilkins or Mrs. Phipps. Not even Miss Tompkins.

Louise was still talking, and her voice ground through Lexie. "Papa said that would be fair since I won, but I'm not supposed to take you from the cabin, Emily Grace. So don't tell anybody."

I hate her, Lexie thought furiously. *I should tell her mother she has the doll on deck.*

But then she heard her own mother's voice in her memory. Mama was saying, "We don't carry tales. That's something a crummy person would do, and you, kiddo, are not a crummy person."

Mama didn't like crummy people. Lexie thought those people were like dumb Doras or bozos, people who didn't care about others. Whatever they were, she was glad Mama didn't think she was one.

She decided not to rush around the corner and fight with Louise. That was another thing a crummy person would do. She was on her way to Mama, after all. Louise didn't matter when Mama would be waiting on the dock in San Francisco.

Mama would probably have rhinestones sparkling on her ears. Maybe she would wear the pretty red top that reached to her hips and the skirt with pleats that swung when she walked. She would be glowing with excitement, so glad to see her daughter again that she would run to the gangway to grab Lexie into a wildly welcoming hug.

Lexie almost ran to the rail to look for the dock and Mama, but the ship was still on the Columbia River though the basalt cliffs of the eastern end were far behind. The forested banks spread wide, with farms here and there. A deer drank briefly from the river's edge before darting back into the trees.

Lexie looked once more at the corner of the wheelhouse and pictured Louise with Emily Grace. "You're not worth the trouble," she whispered. With her head high, she walked back along the deck.

She didn't see Louise again until later that day in the dining salon. With wide eyes, Lexie looked around the vast high-ceilinged room in the middle of the ship. A waiter drew out a cushioned chair for Grandma. Lexie sank into another at a round table covered with a white cloth that draped almost to the polished floor.

As other passengers found their tables, their voices murmuring around her, she traced the gold-banded rim of her china plate. She could hardly believe she was still traveling on a seagoing ship.

An older couple joined them at their table. They seemed used to dining aboard and, after greeting Grandma and smiling at Lexie, began discussing menu choices. Moments later, a tall man with worried brown eyes and an unsmiling little girl of about five took the remaining two seats. The man sat next to Grandma. He introduced himself as Mr. James and his daughter as Millicent. When Grandma tried to speak to the girl, the father said quietly, "Millicent has decided not to speak for a while. Her mother . . . There was an accident. We lost her. I'm taking Millie to her grandparents in San Francisco."

Grandma murmured sympathetically. Lexie wanted to tell Millicent that she knew how she felt, but she didn't think she should call around Grandma and Mr. James. Millicent wasn't listening, anyway. She had her face pressed against her father's sleeve.

Then Louise, her complexion a yellowish color, sat with her mother at the next table, and Lexie forgot about Millicent. The elegant dining salon had almost made her forget how angry she was with Louise. Suddenly she remembered again.

"My goodness," Grandma said with a glance their way. "I'm afraid Louise doesn't take well to ship travel."

Maybe Louise would lose her lunch among all this elegance and embarrass herself and her mother. If that was a vengeful thought, Lexie didn't care. But she didn't say it out loud.

Mrs. Wilkins had the kind of sharp voice that made you listen whether you wanted to or not, and her comments came clearly to their table. "Louise, do not watch other people eat. Sit straight. And take small bites. Remember, you are a Wilkins and a lady."

"She doesn't get a chance to forget that," Lexie whispered while a waiter poured tea for the adults.

Grandma picked up her teacup. "Fortunately, we need not concern ourselves with Louise or her mother."

"Because Lewis ladies don't do that," Lexie said.

Grandma covered her smile behind her napkin, but it glinted in her eyes. "Exactly," she said when she had her voice under control.

Mrs. Wilkins said in a tone she probably thought reached only Louise, "Your outside fork, Louise. You know a dinner fork is not for salad."

Memory struck, and Lexie said softly, "Mama's mother must have been a lot like Mrs. Wilkins. Mama said she got so tired of trying to be perfect for her mama that she gave up and just did whatever worked for her."

Grandma looked startled. After a moment, she said, "She still does. That explains a lot."

"She said she wouldn't raise me like that," Lexie added. "She said I was already the bee's knees just being me."

Grandma sipped her tea, then replaced the delicate china cup in its saucer. "You're doing very well being you," she said, looking straight into Lexie's eyes. "Most folks couldn't ask for better."

Lexie's heart filled with too much warmth to leave room for an answer, but Grandma didn't seem to expect one. She had turned to a waiter to ask how the salmon was prepared.

By the time lunch was finished, the river had grown so wide, the shores were far away at either side. "We're nearing the bar," Grandma said. "It's going to be rough while we cross the surf into the ocean. We'll wait in our stateroom."

"Can't I watch?" Lexie asked, picturing waves crashing into the ship's bow.

Grandma left no room for argument. "No. You may not."

After all the warnings, Lexie felt let down by the bar crossing. She had expected the ship to bounce up and down and maybe lurch from side to side. But this was no fishing trawler. The ship was big and heavy and simply plowed through the surf. She might have felt jolts if she had been at the bow, but the lack of thrill-ride action in their stateroom disappointed her.

Later, while Grandma rested, Lexie asked if she could walk on deck again.

"Wear your hat," Grandma warned, somehow seeing with her eyes closed that Lexie was bareheaded. "And if it starts to rain, come inside before you catch your death."

Lexie pulled her knit cap over her hair, then carefully wrapped the pink knit scarf around Annie. "Wait until you see the ocean," she told the doll. "It goes on forever, all gray and bumpy, with the tops of the waves blowing away in the wind."

Remembering Louise with Emily Grace, Lexie walked forward toward the bridge and looked around the corner. She didn't expect to see Louise, but she was there, sitting on a coil of rope with tears streaming down her face.

Lexie thought about walking away but couldn't bring herself to do that. She tucked Annie into her coat. She didn't need to hear Louise's opinion of a hand-sewn cloth doll. Then she stepped into sight to ask, "Should I get help? Are you sick?"

Louise scrubbed her sleeve across her face. "I hate this ship. My stomach churns all the time. And Emily Grace is *gone!*"

CHAPTER 24

Gone!" Lexie felt sure her heart had dropped to her shoes, as if Louise's words had smashed it right out of her chest. Wind whipped across the deck. She clutched Annie tighter beneath her coat.

Louise's nose was running, and tears slid down her face. Lexie hesitated, then offered a hand-kerchief from her pocket. Momentary sympathy faded. "Where is Emily Grace? What do you mean, she's gone?"

"I don't *know*! I got sick. From the water mov-ing all the time." Little hiccups choked Louise between her words. "I put her here. Inside this coil of rope. I had to go to the rail. I thought I would throw up. Then Mama came out and called me for lunch."

She looked at Lexie, her expression tragic. "I had to leave Emily Grace. What else could I do?"

Taking care that Annie didn't slip, Lexie braced her hands on her hips the way Grandma did when she was upset. Rain was coming. She felt it in the damp wind. Maybe they were steaming into a storm. "You left Emily Grace out here? Alone? During the bar crossing!"

Louise began crying again. Lexie didn't have patience for tears. Not with Emily Grace missing. Not with a storm coming. "Stop that. Tell me what happened!"

Still sobbing, Louise said, "I told you. I had to leave her. And then I had to go with Mama to lunch. And when I came back, she was *gone!*"

She began crying harder, leaning forward with her head in her arms across her knees. Lexie looked at her, wondering what to do. Maybe there wasn't anything she could do. Maybe she should just leave Louise here.

Louise looked up, her flushed face glistening with tears. "You have to help me."

"Help you!" Did Louise remember who she was talking to? "You wouldn't even be here if you hadn't stolen my letter! And Emily Grace would be in the hold where she belongs. Why should I help you?"

"Don't you understand? They expect me to look good for them, like their fancy house and their big Packard. I have to be the best at everything because that makes them look better! And now I've ruined it all!"

They? Them?

She meant her parents. Lexie sank onto a crate and resettled Annie inside her coat. *Grandma doesn't worry that something I do might make her look bad,* she told herself. *When she worries, even when she gets cross, Grandpa says it's because she wants me to grow up to be sensible and honest.*

Grandma was stern—sometimes too stern—because she loved her. *Grandma and Grandpa just care about me growing up happy, and that means being a good person inside.*

She looked again at the loneliness and misery on Louise's face and even though she had thought she could never feel that way, she felt sorry for her. She remembered when she had felt like Louise did and thought that living with Grandpa and Grandma, especially Grandma, was the worst thing that could happen.

But they loved her. She knew that now. She had known it when they used the rainy-day money to buy tickets so she could go to San Francisco.

Sympathy vanished. Emily Grace was lost on the deck with rain coming, maybe even a storm. She might have bounced off when they crossed the bar. What if she had rolled over the side? She couldn't let herself think about that. "Why did you even bring her out here?"

Louise should at least have looked ashamed. Instead, her eyes flashed as if someone had done harm to *her*. "Because Mama just let me *look* at her, not *play* with her. 'Don't mess her hair,' she said. 'Don't wrinkle her dress.'"

"She isn't yours to play with," Lexie snapped. "She's for girls in Japan."

"My mother will say I disgraced her. And my father . . . !" Louise put her head on her arms again, her body shaking. "Please help me, Lexie."

I won't feel sorry for Louise, the cheat, Lexie told herself. But she knew that if she had brought Emily Grace on deck and lost her, Grandma would be horrified. Then she would help find the doll, not worry about how bad it would look for the family name if Lexie lost her.

Again, unwanted sympathy for Louise tried to

creep into Lexie's heart. They'd made the same kind of mistake, after all. *I should have told Grandma about taking the doll from Miss Tompkins's room that day. But I didn't know Grandma then, not the way I know her now.*

And somehow her own voice was saying, "Stop crying. We'll find Emily Grace together."

Maybe not together. She corrected herself at once, pulling back. She hadn't forgiven Louise, even if she was sorry for her. If she had to spend time with Louise, the sorry would disappear fast.

"You look one way. I'll look the other." She glanced across the deck at boxes and crates. Finding one small doll on this huge ship seemed impossible. She held Annie tightly through her coat, almost afraid she might get lost, too. "There's a lot to cover, and it's starting to rain."

Through her tears, Louise exclaimed, "I've looked everywhere already!"

"Where?"

"Here. In the rope. Over there by those boxes, in case she bounced out and rolled."

"That's not everywhere. That's not even a start!"

"It's no use. She's gone!"

"You're giving up? You haven't even looked

and you're giving up!" Lexie wanted to grab the other girl, to force her to her feet, to make her *look.* "Emily Grace is on this ship somewhere. Alone!" She had to be. Lexie couldn't even let herself think of Emily Grace falling overboard.

"Louise!" Mrs. Wilkins shrieked from the doorway to the cabins. "Louise Marie Wilkins! Come in out of the rain!"

Louise jolted to her feet as if her mother had pulled her by a rope. "Find her!" she said, and ran toward the cabins.

"You don't give me orders," Lexie yelled. There wasn't any satisfaction in it. Wind whipped her hair and pulled at her coat. What was it doing to the doll?

She looked out at white tips flying from the water. The doll wasn't out there tossing from one to another. What *was* happening to Emily Grace? *Think!*

There weren't any dogs aboard to run off with her. The ship was heaving in the rough waves, but not enough to bounce the doll out. Not if she had really been settled in the coil of rope. Lexie made herself believe that even when they had crossed the bar, the doll wouldn't have bounced overboard. The ropes would have held her.

Unless she was never in the coil. Could Louise have left her on top and lied about it?

Lexie didn't think so. Louise had been too upset to lie about that, too shocked to find Emily Grace gone.

Suppose a sailor had found the doll! He would have put her somewhere safe, wouldn't he? Where? Lexie wondered if she should ask the captain, but she didn't know where to find the captain. And it was raining harder. There was no *time*.

She looked in one direction and then another and then along the rail toward the stern. Her search stopped at the door into the Grand Salon. She said softly to Annie inside her coat, "Wouldn't the Grand Salon be a safe place where everybody would see Emily Grace sooner or later?"

A sailor who found a doll left on deck with rain coming would think of that. He'd know that the owner would come through the Grand Salon eventually.

"She's there! She has to be!" With her heart singing, Lexie ran to the doorway and pushed it open. The salon was a warm space in the heart of the ship, with cushioned chairs around small tables and tufted benches wrapped around gleaming wooden support columns.

And there was Emily Grace, on one of the benches. She was snuggled in the arms of that little girl, Millicent, the one whose mother had died in an accident. While Lexie watched, Millicent kissed Emily Grace's rosy cheek. For the first time since Lexie had met her at lunch, Millicent was smiling.

CHAPTER 25

I have to get the doll back," Lexie whispered to Annie inside her coat. "Emily Grace is going to Japan. And she has to be kept nice. Louise should never have taken her on deck."

Stories ran through Lexie's head as she tried to think of a way to explain what had happened so Millicent's father would give her the doll. *I could say a mean boy grabbed Emily Grace and ran off with her.*

No, she decided just as quickly. Grandma had talked about white lies. They might be told to make a problem better, but they could hurt somebody just the same. Mrs. Phipps had probably thought no one would be hurt when she said Louise's poem was better. But that had hurt. It had hurt a lot!

If it hadn't been for Mrs. Phipps's white lie, Emily Grace would be safe in her box in the ship's hold with the rest of the dolls.

As Lexie hesitated, Millicent's father looked up and saw her. A sad look crossed his face, as if he'd known something unhappy would happen and here it was. "Your name is Electra, isn't it? We met you at lunch. Is this your doll? We knew someone would be looking for her."

Slowly, Lexie crossed the salon. She couldn't help seeing that Millicent held the doll even more tightly.

The father glanced at the girl, then looked at Lexie again. "We found her left in a coil of rope on deck."

His voice said something more. His voice said, *You didn't take care of her and now she's ours.*

"My . . . friend was playing with her," Lexie said. "But she got seasick and put Emily Grace in the rope while she ran to the rail."

The father's expression said he didn't believe her. "Your *friend* should take better care of her toys."

"She was coming right back," Lexie said quickly.

"You probably just missed her. But she's still sick, so I said I'd find Emily Grace."

Again she saw the father's doubts in his eyes. He didn't think there was a friend. He thought Lexie was talking about herself and that she had left the doll alone on deck. Again, she was getting the blame for something Louise had done. It wasn't fair, and she felt heat rush through her. "You saw Louise at lunch, too. At the next table? Looking sick?"

"That girl is your friend?" He frowned slightly, and Lexie remembered talking about Louise with Grandma in a not very friendly way.

"Not exactly," Lexie said, correcting herself. "Louise is in my class at school." She motioned toward the doll. "That's Emily Grace. She's a Friendship Doll. She's going to Japan with almost thirteen thousand other dolls."

Millicent looked around as if she expected to see dolls popping up all over the Grand Salon.

"To Japan?" Mr. James asked.

"Yes," Lexie said. "They're going to a festival in Japan so girls there will know that our lives might be different but that inside we are like them." Mr. James was still frowning, and she tried again to explain. "Miss Tompkins, our teacher, said those girls and their families will remember the friendship, and our countries can be friends, too, even after we all grow up."

"There are thousands of dolls?" Like Millicent, Mr. James looked around the salon.

Lexie wanted to grab Emily Grace and run to her cabin, but she couldn't do that, so she continued to explain. "A lot of them are packed in boxes in the hold. The rest are already in San Francisco. Or they're on their way there. There's going to be a big party to tell the dolls good-bye before they all leave on a ship for Japan."

"But this doll was on deck." Mr. James frowned. She thought he almost believed her, but because of Millicent, he didn't really want to.

Lexie drew a quick breath, wishing Louise were here so she could watch her try to explain. "Emily Grace should be packed away, too, but Louise's mother said she could carry her to San Francisco. She was supposed to keep her in the cabin, but she took her on deck and then she got seasick and left her in the pile of rope."

Millicent's mouth turned down. She held Emily Grace tightly against her chest and watched Lexie as if wondering whether Lexie could catch her if she jumped up and ran. Lexie prepared to grab for the doll if the girl did try to run off with her.

Mr. James said in a cheerful voice that didn't hide his sadness, "Did you hear that, Millie? This doll is important. She's going to travel all the way to Japan!"

Millie held Emily Grace even tighter. She shook her head, not saying anything.

"We'll look up Japan on a map, Millie," her father said gently. "It will be interesting to see how far she is going."

He lifted Emily Grace from his daughter's arms, then spoke to the doll as if she could understand. "Millicent and I wish you well in your worthy endeavor, Emily Grace. Isn't that right, Millie?"

The little girl leaned forward with her face in her hands. Lexie felt awful. This was Louise's fault. Why had she carried the doll on deck? And left her there!

Mr. James held the doll out and Lexie took her, but she couldn't stop looking at Millicent. The little girl's shoulders were trembling. She must be crying silently. She didn't talk. She must not even cry out loud.

While carefully cradling Emily Grace, Lexie

drew Annie from under her coat. She stepped closer to the little girl and held out the hand-sewn doll. "Millie? This is my Annie. She's soft and warm and very kind. And she's used to tears. I had to go live with my grandparents, too, and I cried a lot at first. Annie understood."

Millie raised her head. Her blue eyes shimmered.

"I found out my grandma and grandpa love me," Lexie told her. "And I found out I love them, too. So I don't need Annie so much." She finished in a rush before she could think about what she was doing. "Here. You can have her. You can tell Annie anything. She'll listen and she's very, very loving."

The little girl hesitated, then grabbed Annie and hugged her close, pressing her cheek to the soft yarn hair.

Her father watched for a moment, then said gently, "Annie may be kind, but I think someone here is even kinder. Are you sure you can let her go? As you say, the other doll . . . Emily Grace . . . will be leaving you for Japan."

"It's all right." And somehow it was. It was hard to see Annie all wrapped up in her pink knit scarf and held tightly by the other girl, but watching her made Lexie feel warm inside.

"I have to go," she said. "Grandma will be looking for me, and I need to put Emily Grace back where she belongs."

As Mr. James nodded, Millicent looked up and gave Lexie something better than a spoken thank-you. She wiped tears from her eyes and smiled.

Lexie smiled back, glad she had thought to give Annie to the girl. When she turned toward the door, she was surprised to see Grandma waiting there.

Would she be mad? Lexie wondered suddenly. After all, Grandma was the one who had made Annie in the first place. And she had made the pink scarf after Lexie cut it up to try to make a dress for Emily Grace.

If Grandma was angry, Lexie hoped she wouldn't say anything that Millie and her father might hear. Holding Emily Grace close, she hurried across the salon.

Grandma put one hand on her shoulder as she came close. Her eyes were gentle as she said, "That was generous of you, Electra. I'm proud of you. Grandpa would be, too."

Lexie felt even warmer inside. Looking back at Annie with Millicent didn't hurt quite so much. She began to feel a little embarrassed, too, not sure how to answer Grandma. So as they stepped out on deck, she said, "Well, I had to get Emily Grace back so she can go to Japan."

"Why was that doll out here and not packed with the others?"

"Louise had her." All the unfairness of that rushed back, and Lexie finished, "She told her parents she needed to carry Emily Grace to San Francisco because that would make up for Jack and me ruining her special day!"

Grandma clicked her tongue against her teeth. "I see."

"And then Louise got sick and left Emily Grace on deck and Millicent found her." Lexie finished silently to herself, *And when her mother finds out Louise left the doll on deck, she's going to get in trouble, the way she deserves!*

CHAPTER 26

Lexie took Emily Grace into the cabin to smooth her hair and straighten her skirts. Then she carried the doll down the narrow hallway to Louise's cabin. She enjoyed imagining Louise's face when her mother heard what had happened. She was going to hear it all: the deck, the coil of rope, having to take Emily Grace away from sad little Millicent.

But with every step, her purpose began to fade. What did Louise matter when Mama was waiting in San Francisco? Maybe feeling seasick was punishment enough.

She was still a few steps away when Mrs. Wilkins opened the cabin door and started to step out. Louise's mother stopped when she saw Lexie. "The Friendship Doll? What are you doing with it?"

Louise peeked from the cabin behind her. If anything, she looked even sicker.

"Louise . . ." Lexie hesitated, then went on. "Louise let me hold her for a while. Now it's time for Emily Grace to go back into her box."

"It certainly is." Mrs. Wilkins snatched the doll and turned to her cabin. "Louise! Put this doll away. You were not given permission to let just anyone play with her."

Just anyone? Lexie felt slapped, though she shouldn't have been surprised at anything Mrs. Wilkins decided to say.

"Lexie's not just anyone," Louise said, surprising her. "She's my friend."

No, I'm not! Lexie was glad she didn't say those words aloud. She remembered hearing Louise telling the doll that her friends only cared for the candy she could buy them or that their fathers' jobs depended on her father.

You have to earn friendship, Lexie thought, but maybe Louise had been trying to earn her friendship when she defended Lexie to her mother. *A few days ago, she wouldn't have done that.*

Mrs. Wilkins's mouth took on a pinched look,

but before she could say anything more, Louise got an even stranger expression on her face. Then she threw up.

Lexie jumped back, but it was too late for Mrs. Wilkins. As Lexie hurried away, she couldn't help smiling to herself. After this, Mrs. Wilkins might be more careful about upsetting Louise.

Sleeping in the narrow bunk aboard the ship was strange yet soothing. Lexie enjoyed a sense of floating as she listened to the rush of water against the hull and the distant, powerful rumble of the engine.

All the next morning, she talked with sailors when one could spare a minute, or tossed crumbs to seagulls, or searched the blowing surf in the hope of glimpsing a mermaid. The shoreline slid along— rocky cliffs, houses nestled in coves, small sheltered bays with a few fishing boats, though most were at sea now with their trawling booms lowered.

Everything fascinated Lexie, but part of her mind stayed with Mama.

She pictured the dresses in Mama's closet and mentally took out one after another, remembering when Mama had bought it, where she had worn it, and whether she would choose that one when she came to meet the ship.

Millicent wasn't at breakfast. Her father said she had slept well for the first time since her mother's death. He filled plates for both of them and took them back to his cabin. At lunchtime, they came in together, Millicent cradling Annie in her arms.

When her father seated her, Millicent carefully placed the doll on the chair beside her. The older woman next to her smiled and said, "What a sweet doll you have, dear. What is her name?"

Lexie winced at the reminder that Millie didn't talk. To her surprise, the little girl whispered, "Annie."

Both Grandma and Lexie looked at Millie's father. His eyes glimmered, but he was smiling. "Annie is a very special doll, Electra."

"She is," Lexie said, leaning around Grandma. "My grandma made her for me."

"Then she was made with love. She's exactly what Millie needed."

"I'm glad," Lexie said, and she was glad. She was proud of Annie, too. Annie knew her job and how to do it.

At last, the ship turned toward land. When Lexie stood at the rail watching an inlet grow larger, a sailor paused beside her. "You won't be seeing San

Francisco Bay like this for long. They're planning to build a bridge all the way from the rocks where the city ends to that wild point of land across the channel."

"How can they do that?" Lexie looked at the rough water crashing against the rocks at either side of the wide inlet to the bay. Wouldn't waves sweep away any posts they tried to put in?

"They'll do it," the sailor said before walking on. "They're going to call it the Golden Gate."

"The Golden Gate," Lexie repeated. She thought her eyes must be shining. She was sailing under an almost-bridge called the Golden Gate on her way to Mama. She clutched the rail while they sailed into San Francisco Bay. Seagulls screeched overhead, diving and swooping.

Lexie held the rail even tighter. She ached for her first glimpse of Mama.

Ships of all sizes crowded the piers that jutted into the bay. Some had funnels. Masts rose from others, their sails furled. Excitement ran through all the passengers. The sense of waiting was over. People were gathering possessions and looking for newly made friends to say good-bye or to make plans to meet in the future.

Everyone seemed to be talking at once. If

possible, the excitement ran even higher as the ship eased to a space along a pier. Lexie squeezed over to make room for Grandma at the rail. "She'll be wearing the pleated skirt and red top," she told Grandma. "I've thought of all her outfits, and that's what she'll choose to wear. Because she knows it's my favorite."

Grandma smiled and patted her hand. Lexie couldn't stay still. She bounced on her toes as she looked from people crowding the rail to the throngs on the dock.

People filled the wharf, waving, calling out, hurrying back and forth. People on the ship shouted and waved, too. The shouts on ship and shore got louder whenever anyone spotted a friend or relative.

Lexie waved and shouted with the rest while she searched the people on the dock below. "Mama! Where are you? Do you see me? Wave if you do! I'm up here!"

The noise crowded around her with the people. Gradually, Lexie became a silent island in the middle of it all. Mama was there somewhere. But she couldn't see her. Lexie leaned hard against the rail, as if that would get her closer to the dock.

The crew finished settling a gangplank in place. At last, passengers were allowed to go ashore. Lexie saw Louise and her mother pushing to the front of the line. Louise would be glad to feel solid ground beneath her feet.

Never mind Louise. Lexie swept her gaze across the people on the dock again and again. So many people. So many strangers. She wanted to see Mama before joining all those people. Where was she?

Fear swelled inside. Lexie knew her voice sounded shrill. She didn't care. She wanted to scream like a three-year-old. "I don't see her! Where's Mama? Where is she?"

The entire world had narrowed down to a crowded dock that to Lexie looked horribly empty. "Grandma, I can't see her! *Where is my mama?*"

CHAPTER 27

Lexie screamed again, "Mama!"

Grandma's hand came warm and solid on her shoulder. "That flapper! I might have known—" She stopped herself, then said with an obvious effort to be patient, "She's been delayed, I expect."

"Delayed?" Tears blurred Lexie's eyes as she tried to look at Grandma.

"Something's held her up. You know your mama. It's always the last minute with her." Grandma turned toward the gangplank. "By the time we sort out our luggage, no doubt she'll find us."

Mama should be here now. Something must have happened to her. A sick feeling shivered down through Lexie. She couldn't leave the rail.

On the dock, a marching band played bouncy music that should have made her feet dance. Lexie stood as if glued to the deck, searching past the band and through the crowds, hoping for a glimpse of Mama.

"Come along," Grandma said in her no-nonsense voice. "We'll join the others collecting luggage."

"If we leave the rail, she might not see us."

"She'll see us." Impatience edged into Grandma's words. "Come along, Electra."

They threaded past crew members carrying luggage onto the dock. When Lexie and Grandma located theirs among the rest, Mama still had not come. Grandma sat on her trunk while Lexie walked restlessly back and forth. Sailors shouted as they worked cranes to lower freight. Seagulls swooped and screeched. She felt as if her thoughts were swooping and screeching right along with the gulls.

Hope lifted briefly when her steps carried her near the ticket office, but Mama wasn't there, either. What if Mama was hurt? What if a motorcar had hit her while she was running to the dock?

Grandma would say, "Never borrow trouble."

Lexie made herself study a travel poster with a picture of a Japanese temple and a young woman in her kimono. And her obi, she told herself. *Obi* was what Miss Tompkins called the wide sash wrapped around the kimono's middle and folded in a huge bow at the back. The narrow sash like a rope that went around the obi and held the big bow in place was the *obi-jime*.

The poster said, *Come and visit the Land of the Rising Sun.* Then there were a lot of words in different languages that might have said the same thing. Lexie wished she had Emily Grace with her, so she could show the doll where she would be going. The poster said the people in Japan wanted visitors. That must mean they would be happy to welcome Emily Grace and the other dolls.

She looked around for Louise, wondering if she still had the doll with her, but Louise and her mother had gone. Millicent and her father stood a short distance away with an older couple, all of them sharing hugs and tears.

Lexie tried to feel happy for Millie, but deep inside, she envied the little girl. She should be caught into Mama's arms by now. Mama should be saying, "There you are, kiddo! I've missed you like crazy! We'll never be apart again!"

She would be here. She would be. She was just delayed, like Grandma said; that was all.

Slowly Lexie walked to Grandma, but she couldn't resist looking back at Millicent and her family. Mr. James and the older man were loading luggage into the trunk of a big black car with soaring fenders and wide running boards. When Millie looked over and saw Lexie watching, she waved, holding Annie close.

Lexie fought back a wrench of regret. *Annie!* How could she have given away her doll?

Mr. James glanced around, then said something to the others before walking over to Grandma. "Is someone meeting you, Mrs. Lewis?"

"Thea . . . my daughter-in-law . . . has apparently been delayed," Grandma answered. "I see your family found you."

"Yes." He glanced toward the others, but his forehead creased. "Your daughter-in-law may have sent a message. Have you asked the ticket agent?"

Relief flooded Grandma's face. She lurched to her feet. "I hadn't thought of it. I'll do that right now."

Mr. James gestured for her to sit back on the trunk. "Please. Allow me." Before Grandma could argue, he strode across the dock to the crowded office.

"It never crossed my mind," Grandma told Lexie. "The agent will have a telephone. Your mother may have called."

There will be a message. Relief swept through Lexie. *Mama wouldn't leave us sitting here wondering what to do next.*

Minutes later, Mr. James returned with a folded paper in one hand. Lexie's heart leaped. There was a message. Of course there was. She saw Grandma's name written across the top. Mr. James waited while Grandma opened the note.

"She's joining people for an early supper," Grandma said slowly. "She wants us to meet her at the restaurant. Here's the address." Grandma looked from the note to Lexie. "My stars, does she expect us to carry our luggage on our backs?"

"There's ample space in my parents' town car," Mr. James said. "It will be our pleasure to transport you and your luggage to Lexie's mother."

"We can't take you out of your way," Grandma exclaimed.

Lexie wanted to protest, *Yes, we can!* She tugged at Grandma's sleeve. "They have room, Grandma."

Mr. James looked toward the town car again. Millie stood beside the front fender with her grandmother's arm around her. It looked like Millie was giving one- or two-word answers to the older woman, but she was talking. She wasn't stuck in silence like before.

Tears glimmered in Mr. James's eyes when he turned again to Grandma. "I can never repay the debt you are owed. Please let us do this small favor."

Grandma nodded, rising to her feet. "If our little homemade doll has helped Millicent, that is payment enough for us. But we will accept your kind offer."

"Thank you." He hoisted Grandma's trunk to one shoulder and took Lexie's suitcase in his free hand. They followed him along the dock. While he lowered the luggage into the open trunk, Lexie climbed into the car's backseat with Millie and Grandma. Mr. James joined his parents up front. He half turned to smile back at Millie, as if afraid she might forget how to talk again if he took his eyes off her for long.

Mama's going to look at me like that, Lexie told herself. *She'll be so glad to see me, she won't be able to stop looking at me and smiling.*

The older Mr. James cranked down his window and rested one arm on the sill while the salty-scented air blew in, mixed with the exhaust of motorcars and the smell of coal smoke. To Lexie, Portland seemed a small town compared to San Francisco.

The waterfront bustled with ships unloading and people rushing everywhere. The city streets were even more thronged. She couldn't see the tops of buildings on either side of the car. When she looked ahead through the front window, she saw buildings farther away, soaring into the sky. Could they really find Mama in this big, busy city?

The fluttery feeling in her stomach said they could. It said they were almost to her. Mama must have had a good reason for not meeting the ship. The people she was with were important. Soon she would tell Lexie all about it.

Maybe those people were important to Toby. The thought hit suddenly. Toby had insisted that Mama come with him to the restaurant. That made sense. It was Toby's fault. It wasn't Mama's choice to leave Lexie waiting at the ship. It was Toby. That was just like him. She remembered him saying that children didn't belong with people who worked at night and slept all day. Toby didn't want kids around at all.

Lexie put her disappointment and hurt into one big bundle with Toby's name on top. Being left to find their way from the ship didn't matter when it was Toby's fault. And soon she would be with Mama.

Thinking that made Lexie feel better. But she wondered how Mama, who had been married to wonderful Papa, had ever chosen Toby.

They drove up a hill and down again and past a park in a big square where ladies pushed baby buggies, children ran about, and a band played. Enormous hotels and department stores cast long shadows. Before Lexie could see everything, Mr. James turned onto a side street and drove several more blocks.

The streets were quieter here, lined with small businesses. From curtains in windows above and flowerpots on some of the sills, Lexie guessed people must live on the higher floors.

"There's your street address," Millie's grandpa

called over his shoulder. "There on the right with the dark-purple awning."

Lexie leaned forward to peer through the front window, her heart pounding so hard she almost thought it would leap out of her chest.

CHAPTER 28

Millie's grandpa pulled the big town car into a space right in front of the purple awning. Her father stepped out and came back to open the car door.

As Lexie followed Grandma out, a door swung open below the awning. Mama rushed through. Her eyes matched the sparkle of her rhinestone earrings, and she was wearing the red top and pleated skirt that seemed to swing even when she was still. "You're here! At last, kiddo! I've missed you so much!"

Lexie fought happy tears. She clung to Mama, hugging her just as she had meant to do on the dock after running from the ship into her arms.

Lexie could feel Mama's energy vibrating through her. Her eyes sparkled. Her skirt pleats danced.

Lexie remembered Toby saying, "Your mama never lets a minute pass her by without catching hold of it with both hands." Grandma said an ordinary person got exhausted just being around her.

That was Mama. Sometimes she forgot to eat or sweep the floor, but she was more fun than anybody, and Lexie couldn't think of anything better than being together again.

Mama hugged Grandma next and looked like she might hug Mr. James, but he looked startled and took a step back.

"Thea," Grandma said, "Mr. James and his parents were kind enough to drive us from the dock. We have luggage."

Lexie heard scolding in Grandma's voice, but Mama didn't seem to notice. "The super will take care of it." She darted to a door next to the restaurant and called inside, "They're here!" then rushed back to Lexie. "Your stuff will be taken up to my place. It's all arranged."

With a grin, she shook hands with Mr. James, then leaned into the car to thank his parents. Lexie waved to Millie in the backseat. She had known the little girl for only a short time, but it was sad to think she wouldn't see her again.

Softly Millie said, "Good-bye."

Hearing Millie speak, even if it was just one word, made it easier for Lexie to give up her doll. "Annie's going to be good company, Millie. You tell her when you need a hug."

Millie's father pressed Lexie's shoulder, then climbed into the car with his parents. As Lexie watched them drive away, Mama turned, almost dancing with happiness. "It's nifty to see you again, kiddo. Mother Lewis, it's really swell of you to bring her to me. Come on inside, both of you."

"How big is your apartment?" Lexie asked. "Is it on the second floor? Do you have a good view?"

Mama laughed. "You'll see it soon enough, kiddo. First I want you and your grandma to meet my new friends!"

Lexie didn't want to meet anyone new. She had a hundred — a hundred hundred — things to tell Mama and questions to ask. But when Mama opened the restaurant door, the rich smells of clam chowder and the tangy scent of the bread Lexie knew was called sourdough reached out and pulled her right on in.

She looked around but didn't see Toby. He must be playing in a band somewhere. Maybe he would be away for a long time. She hoped so.

A man rose to his feet at the nearest table while a woman beside him smiled at them. The man looked solid, with wavy red hair parted in the middle and a neat red mustache. Beneath the mustache, he offered a wide grin. "So this is your little girl. I see the resemblance. Welcome. Welcome!"

Mama gave Lexie a little push forward. "This is Lexie. And Mrs. Lewis. Mother Lewis, meet Mr. Clayton and—"

The man broke in. "Harold Clayton, photographer. Call me Hal. Everybody does. And here's my better half, Sylvia."

Mrs. Clayton seemed nice, with kind eyes and a friendly smile. She wore a brown dress and a neat brown cloche with trim brown hair curling from beneath. *She's brown all over,* Lexie thought, amused. *Like a mouse, a friendly one.*

Mrs. Clayton looked at her husband in the fond way most folks looked at a puppy or a kitten. "The mister doesn't put much stock in formality."

Mama laughed. "You two! Aren't you the bee's knees!" She urged Lexie and Grandma into chairs at the table as a waitress came over with menus. Grandma murmured hello to the couple, but Lexie didn't hear much enthusiasm in her voice.

It didn't matter. They were here, together with Mama again.

Mama reached under her chair. "I have a surprise for you, kiddo." She put a wrapped package in front of Lexie. "One of the gals at the club makes these. The moment I saw them, I knew I had to get one for you!"

"What is it?" Lexie felt her smile getting even wider as she pulled off the string and opened the paper. A doll lay inside, a soft-bodied lady doll, tall and thin, with a painted face, a column of a flapper dress, and a long pearl necklace. A glittery headband held her bobbed brown hair.

"Isn't she a kick?" Mama asked.

"I love her!" Lexie held the doll up for everyone to see, then hugged her close. "She's a grown-up Annie! I'm going to call her Ann."

Grandma explained, "Lexie gave her cloth doll, Annie, to a lonely little girl on the ship."

Everyone had something nice to say about giving away Annie and how pretty the new doll was. Then Mama said, "Guess what! Hal and Sylvia are going to Japan with the dolls!"

Lexie looked at the couple in surprise. "On the ship?"

"That's right, Miss Lexie." Mr. Clayton dropped his menu to the table. "I work for magazines. You may have seen a travel poster at the dock, one with a geisha in her kimono with a temple in the background? The Japanese are reaching out for tourists. So one of my magazines is sending us to make a photo spread of the country."

"You'll be a long way from home," Grandma said, sounding as if she wasn't sure travel was a good thing.

"A lot of people are making the trip," Hal said, beaming. "Those with money to spare. Charlie Chaplin went over. And that writer fellow . . . Hemingway."

Mama's eyes sparkled. "Hal's going to take pictures of the ceremony tomorrow. Guess what, kiddo? You and I might turn up in his magazine!"

Hal chuckled. "My better half came up with that idea. I'll shoot pictures of the big send-off here and then of the welcome the dolls get in Yokohama."

"I expect you will focus on the dolls, not on people," Grandma said. Lexie knew Grandma hoped it would be that way. She wouldn't approve of Mama and Lexie turning up in pictures in a magazine. To Sylvia, Grandma added politely, "It is an interesting idea."

Sylvia's fair skin turned pink. "I see picture possibilities sometimes. The mister is the artist."

The waitress set bowls brimming with chowder in front of each of them, then returned with a big basket of bread. Lexie was glad she had food and the new doll Ann to think about, because Mr. Clayton took over the conversation, talking about things called apertures and lenses and light and other stuff the grown-ups might have found interesting but was boring as anything to her.

When Mama finally led her with Grandma to the apartment house next door, Lexie felt her curiosity come back to life. The first thing she noticed was Mama's spicy scent, as if the small corner apartment reached out to hug her the same way Mama had. She looked through both windows at the lighted streets, marveling all over again that she was actually here in San Francisco.

The luggage waited just inside the door. "Isn't this the cat's meow!" Mama said, twirling in the center of the room. "This little place brings us all close together."

"Like a family," Lexie said meaning, *like a family should be.* Grandma didn't say anything.

Mama helped Lexie tug Grandma's trunk into the bedroom. "We'll share the sofa, kiddo," she said. "The back drops down, so we'll have oodles of room."

After two warnings from Grandma, Lexie stopped asking questions long enough to unpack her nightgown. Grandma raised her eyebrows. "Goodness, you have enough in your suitcase for a long stay."

That was because she meant to be here for a long stay, but it brought another question to mind. Lexie asked, "Where's Toby? Is he playing his horn somewhere?"

She hoped he didn't come in late and trip over the open sofa or, worse, accidentally climb into bed with Grandma! She just managed to swallow a giggle. Grandma wouldn't think that was funny.

Mama answered lightly. "He's down in Hollywood — can you beat that? Friends of his hooked up with an outfit playing background music for the flicks and invited him along."

"Flicks?" Grandma asked.

"Moving pictures," Lexie explained, trying to

keep a leap of happiness out of her voice. Mama didn't seem disappointed that Toby was gone.

"I'm surprised you stayed behind," Grandma told her.

Sudden understanding left Lexie feeling bruised inside. Toby was gone. He hadn't kept Mama away from the ship. She and Grandma could still be sitting there alone on the dock and it wouldn't be Toby's fault after all.

It had to be his fault. There was no one else to blame . . . no one she was willing to blame. Maybe there was. Maybe it was Mr. Clayton's fault. Hadn't she thought that earlier?

Rhinestones flashed in Mama's ears as she answered Grandma. "They don't have need for a songbird. Guess they don't want to distract people from the story going on in the flicks."

She came over to Lexie, looking as if Toby were in the past and didn't matter anymore. "I have something swell to tell you, kiddo, but it's got to be a secret until after the dolls' send-off. I don't want your thoughts pulled two ways, and we need to practice our song."

A secret from Mama would be something exciting. Mama didn't care much about boring things.

All that talk about photography had come close to boring, but Mama's mind was probably far off on something else, something secret, all the time Mr. Clayton was chattering on. Maybe the photographer and his wife were part of the secret and that's why they kept Mama from meeting the ship!

Lexie didn't mind waiting to hear Mama's news. A secret from her was like a Christmas present all wrapped up under a sparkly tree like the ones they made when they spent Christmas together. A lot of the fun with a present was in wondering what could be inside.

With Mama, it could be anything. A kitten. Or a jack-in-the-box that jumped up the minute she opened the package. Or maybe . . . just maybe . . . it was a promise that from now on, Lexie would live with her all the time. It would be worth waiting for. She was sure of that.

CHAPTER 29

Light rain blew on the wind the next day when they walked to the pier where the dolls' farewell would be held. As Grandma pulled her scarf tighter, Mama said with a grin, "Nifty weather for January."

Lexie twirled in a circle, laughing. "It's great weather! We're together!" They'd had fun practicing "The Blue-Eyed Doll" over and over last night. She became so sleepy, she hardly knew what she was singing, but every minute had been like a party.

Now, with the wind blowing and waves slapping the piers, she felt wide awake. She skipped between Mama and Grandma as they walked down the dock to join the photographer and his wife. Grandma talked to Mrs. Clayton while Mr. Clayton steadied his big black camera on a tall tripod. The ship waited nearby, an enormous oceangoing freighter far longer than the ship they had taken from Portland.

Men rushed along the wharf, shouting orders, setting lines, and moving crates from the dock up to the ship to be stored in the hold. Emily Grace would travel to Japan on that ship. Suddenly, the dolls' trip was real, not just a school project.

"What do you think of her, kiddo?" Mama asked, swinging Lexie's hand.

"It's big." Maybe she should say, *she's big,* but it seemed silly to think of a black freighter almost as long as the pier as a she.

"They say five of these ships have offered space to carry the dolls."

"Why do they need five?" Lexie exclaimed. That big ship could hold her entire schoolhouse!

"Twelve thousand and more dolls take up a lot of space," Mama said. "Remember, each one travels in a box big enough to hold her suitcase and all her trappings."

Grandma added, "I'm sure each ship carries a lot of paying cargo besides."

Lexie walked backward, watching sailors work. "Is this one going to carry Emily Grace?"

"Could be, kiddo." Mama sounded distant, and Lexie saw that she was watching a handsome man in a uniform walking from the gangplank. "There's Captain Richards. I need to talk to him. Back in a sec."

As Mama walked toward the captain, the photographer said, "Your mother is like a beam of sunlight. She lights up everything around her. I hope I can get that quality into my photos."

Lexie had forgotten that he was going to take photos of them singing together. She felt a little jealous that he was watching Mama and that the captain looked happy to see her. It was like little parts of Mama were being taken away by other people, when Lexie wanted her all to herself.

Mama brought the captain over for introductions. The Claytons already knew him, since they were sailing to Japan on his ship. His smile was friendly and he seemed nice, but Lexie didn't want to stand around talking. "They're about to start the dolls' party," she reminded Mama.

"We'd better nip on inside," Mama agreed. "Captain Richards is coming with us, so we can count on a friendly audience."

"I look forward to it," he said.

Lexie reminded herself that no matter how he smiled at Mama, he was leaving very soon to sail away to Japan.

Mr. Clayton collected his camera gear, and they all went into a nearby hall where people were gathering. Mama spotted four seats together near the front and rushed ahead to save them while the photographer and his wife carried their equipment to a spot near the stage.

Lexie looked around. Huge paper flowers along the walls brightened the hall. An enormous painting of Mount Fuji made a background for the stage, with a tall model of a Japanese temple at one side and papier-mâché trees bristling with blossoms at the other.

Three young women in flowered kimonos moved through the crowd, offering programs and helping people find seats. Their hair was styled like that of the woman in the travel poster and decorated with sprays of flowers and ribbons.

"Those women aren't Japanese," Lexie said.

"I don't suppose the program committee could hire Japanese women," Grandma answered. "You've heard Grandpa talk about the law passed two years ago. People from their country aren't allowed to immigrate here anymore."

"Why?"

"There's fear newcomers will take all the jobs and leave our people without work."

People were expecting a lot of Emily Grace and the others, Lexie told herself. She couldn't help wondering if even twelve thousand dolls could make people from different countries become friends.

Where *was* Emily Grace? Lexie rose on her toes to look ahead through the crowd. Below the painting of Mount Fuji, row after row of dolls sat or stood facing the audience.

Beside her, Grandma said, "My goodness, most are dressed like little girls, but look at those two on the end. A bride and groom!"

"Maybe they're supposed to be children playing dress-up," Lexie suggested.

"Huh. I can't say I've ever met a ten- or eleven-year-old boy willing to dress up as a groom."

Lexie giggled, picturing Jack Harmon dressed like that. While Grandma joined Mama and Captain Richards, Lexie walked to the stage and looked at the dolls. Her breath caught in her throat when she saw Emily Grace near the middle.

She leaned closer, longing to hold the doll once more and wish her good luck in Japan.

A flashlamp blazed nearby. Lexie blinked at the white light and turned almost blindly in the resulting smoke, managing to make out Mr. Clayton with his camera on its tripod.

"Perfect," he said. "The look on your face spoke of all the hope and love and longing put into these dolls by the children of America. Sylvia suggested the shot, and she was right." He beamed at his wife. "My idea girl. Don't know what I'd do without her."

Sylvia's cheeks reddened. "I like a picture that tells a story."

"Sir!" Mrs. Wilkins steamed up with Louise in tow. "If you are photographing girls who are part of this project, you need my daughter. She won a contest for writing the best letter to accompany the doll from her class."

Lexie felt as if someone had just kicked to life a hot ember in her stomach. Fire flared through her. Then she saw Louise's face and some of the flames died down. Louise looked as if she couldn't decide whether to cry or to run.

"Well, then, young lady," Mr. Clayton said, "step on up here beside your friend."

I'm not her friend! Lexie bit the words back.

Louise's cheeks were bright red. Her eyes were bright, too. Sounding defiant, she said, "I had to write the best letter. Or Mother and Father would stop loving me. Because I always have to be the best for them."

"Louise!" Mrs. Wilkins exclaimed, patting the bird on her hat and looking flustered. "What a silly thing to say."

"But I couldn't write the best letter," Louise said in a rush. "Because Lexie did. I didn't know what to do, so I took hers and said it was mine."

Mrs. Wilkins's face got as red as Louise's. "You don't know what you're saying!"

"I do know," Louise said. "I can't think of anything else. I think that's why I got sick on the ship. And when I get back to school, I'll tell everybody the truth."

Her mother looked horrified, but Louise blinked away the tears shining in her eyes and kept on as if she couldn't stop the words once she'd started. "Lexie helped me on the ship and didn't get mad when I lost Emily Grace and I heard she even gave away the doll her grandma made her to get Emily Grace back. And I don't think I could have done that. But I think I can tell the truth about what I did do."

Mrs. Wilkins looked around as if hoping her real daughter would suddenly appear. Or maybe she just needed somewhere to sit down. "Well, I never." Even the bird on her hat seemed to droop. "I never," she said again, as if a full sentence were out of her reach.

Her mouth trembling, Louise looked at her mother. "I'm sorry, Mama."

Mrs. Wilkins's color had faded until her skin turned pale. She looked as if she were seeing Louise for the first time. Maybe she was seeing herself through Louise's eyes, Lexie thought, feeling uncomfortable with the tension between them.

"I suspect we're both sorry," Mrs. Wilkins said then, her voice quiet. "We're going to need a long talk. We'll both think about this while they start the program."

Lexie grabbed Louise's hand. The girl's misery made tears behind her own eyes. "You collected more money to buy and dress the doll than anybody else in the class. And you brought her all the way here."

She turned to Mr. Clayton. "You should take a picture of us both." She glanced at Mrs. Clayton, the photographer's "idea girl," and added, "We're both part of the doll's story."

"Of course you are!" Mrs. Clayton bustled them to the front of the stage and began positioning them. Lexie was glad to be distracted by posing and not to have to say anything.

She wasn't sure she forgave Louise, who had done her a terrible wrong. But she wasn't mad anymore. Not too mad, anyway. It would take a lot of courage for Louise to tell the truth at school. If she found the strength to do that, maybe they could learn to be friends. Or at least not enemies.

Lexie brought her thoughts to a fast stop. It wouldn't matter. She wouldn't be at school. She was here with Mama, and she meant to stay. The school and everyone she knew there were part of her past. She wasn't going to change her mind now that she and Mama were finally together. Not for Grandpa and Grandma. Nor for Jack. Regret shivered through her, but she pushed it away.

The photographer advanced the film in his camera and adjusted his lens. Lexie tried to brace for the flash, but again it almost blinded her. As someone on the stage tested the microphone, she blinked, trying to see, then made her way to her seat beside Grandma.

A woman walked to the microphone to welcome the audience and tell them how the doll project had come about and how children by themselves or in groups had saved their money to buy 12,739 dolls to send to Japan. The audience clapped loudly and another flash blazed.

When it was time for Lexie and Mama to sing "The Blue-Eyed Doll," Lexie walked up to the microphone to explain the song first, the way they'd practiced. Her amplified voice startled her at first. She moved back a little and began again. "Our song was written by a Japanese poet in 1921. It is about a celluloid doll that arrived in Japan aboard a freighter. The doll had blue eyes and blond hair, and the song asks the Japanese girls to be her friends. 'The Blue-Eyed Doll' is popular in Japan. We hope our dolls will be loved, too."

She stepped back beside Mama, then remembered to speak into the microphone again to add, "We will be singing the song in English."

As she joined Mama and waited for the music to begin, Lexie looked out at the audience. Millie sat near her father with Annie on her lap. She leaned closer to say something to him. He smiled back with so much love that Lexie's heart gave an aching wrench.

Millie's father was smiling at Millie the way Papa had once smiled. Lexie missed Papa so suddenly and deeply that she wondered if she would be able to sing. Then the music came up, and the words came to her lips just the way they had with Mama last night. Their voices blended well together as always, but Lexie heard sadness in her own. She knew her longing for Papa came through the song.

A moment of silence followed. She wondered if she had ruined the song by feeling sad. Then the crowd roared with applause. Flashes flared from several cameras, making it hard to see people in the audience through the smoke. Mama took her hand as they left the stage to find their seats. "Kiddo, you are a star!"

CHAPTER 30

Everyone they passed smiled or said something like "Beautiful" or "I loved your song." Lexie was glad to take the empty seat beside Grandma and feel her comfortable warmth nearby while people turned in their seats to smile.

Women in kimonos rushed on stage, taking fast little steps in *geta*s, the wooden clogs on little wooden bars that held them above the floor. They looked like dancing dolls to Lexie as they performed with parasols and fans. Then children ran on to kick a heavy leather ball into the air and try to keep it from touching the floor.

Lexie looked at her program and saw that the game was called *kemari* and had come to Japan from China in the sixth century. Drummers performed next, their beats stirring through Lexie until she bounced in her seat.

A Japanese woman who had immigrated to San Francisco before the law changed came on stage to sing a high-pitched trilling song. Lexie sat still, hearing each clear note like the ring of a wet fingertip around the rim of one of Grandma's best crystal goblets.

She clapped and cheered for every performance until she felt hoarse and was glad her own song had come early in the program. All the while, in a part of her mind, she thought about Mama's surprise and tried to guess what it might be.

The excitement and applause still echoed through her as she settled into a seat at a crowded table in a restaurant on the waterfront. Captain Richards had to go back to his ship, but the Claytons joined them. Everyone talked at once. Lexie managed to catch Grandma's attention. "Millie and her father were there. Did you see them?"

"I didn't. I'm glad they came."

"She looked happy."

Grandma nodded, but she studied Lexie with troubled eyes. Maybe she had understood the sadness when Lexie sang.

"Here, now," Mr. Clayton said. "You don't look like a girl who just wowed everybody with a song."

His wife smiled. "Or like a girl about to go on the greatest adventure of her life."

Mama laughed. "That's because she doesn't know yet!"

"Know what?" Lexie looked at Mama with excitement rushing through her again. Was it finally time for the surprise?

"Hal and Sylvia invited me to share their travels to Japan! I knew that passport would come in handy someday. Everyone said I was nuts to get one."

Lexie's stomach plummeted to her toes. "Japan," she repeated. That was the surprise? Her voice sounded as sick as she felt. She had planned to be with Mama forever. But she couldn't stay in San Francisco alone. "When will you come back?"

Mrs. Clayton looked flustered. "I thought she knew. I'm sorry!"

"Don't be. It's time to spill the beans." Mama reached past Grandma to clasp Lexie's hand. "Hal and Sylvia invited me to travel with them and help set up photographs. They say I have a way with people."

"People cotton to your mama," Mr. Clayton said. "We've been a little worried the women in Japan won't want to pose. But your mama can talk anyone into anything!"

"But . . . when will you come back?" Lexie struggled to swallow tears before they could reach her eyes.

Mama's sparkle looked even brighter. "That's the wrong question, kiddo. You should ask when will *we* come back."

"We?" Lexie felt even more confused. Did Mama mean the Claytons? It didn't matter when they came back. But Mama . . . How could Mama go away now, when they'd just gotten together?"

"Oh, Thea," Grandma said, the words coming out like a moan.

"You don't get it, do you, kiddo? Grandma does. You're going to Japan with us! Since we're mother and daughter, you can travel on my passport."

To Japan? With Mama! That was the surprise! Mama had missed meeting the ship because she was arranging for them to travel together. Lexie's wheeling thoughts made her feel dizzy.

Mama laughed at Lexie's expression. "You can

thank Captain Richards. When I told him how you and I used to sing together in restaurants in Seattle, he offered free passage to you as well as to me if we'll sing to his passengers and crew in the evenings!"

"Captain Richards?" Lexie asked. "It was his idea for us both to go?"

"He said we'd be a pair of canaries!" Mama said.

"Her schooling," Grandma protested, sounding as if she was gearing up for a serious argument.

Mama waved it away before it could begin. "How many little girls steam away to Japan, Mother Lewis? Lexie's going to pick up a nifty education. Travel. People. Places. She'll see a part of the world most girls only read about!"

Mr. Clayton put in, "It's a great opportunity."

Japan, Lexie told herself. Where people had mats on their floors instead of carpets and paper for walls. It was going to be an adventure.

But no matter how much she thought about it, she just felt numb. Mama wasn't leaving her after all. Mama was taking her along to Japan. She should be excited. She *was* excited, but she also saw Grandma looking as if she might become ill.

This is me, my life. Grandma has to understand.

Mama kept talking about all the nifty things they would see in Japan and the keen people they would meet, with the Claytons adding their ideas. "And just think," Mama finished. "We'll get to watch the ceremony welcoming the dolls to Japan! Won't that be the berries? You don't have to say good-bye to Emily Grace. You're going with her!"

"Sylvia has some great ideas for photographs," Mr. Clayton said.

His wife added, "The mister will photograph the adventure of one girl and her doll leaving America to be welcomed in Japan. It will make a wonderful story!"

Lexie felt strange: excited and scared at the same time. She couldn't help remembering that this was Captain Richards's idea. Mama might have left her here with Grandma.

Hal chuckled as if he saw that thought in Lexie's eyes. "Grandma will get her life back."

That was a mistake. Grandma saw a chance to aim her anger and took it. "If you think for one moment I haven't enjoyed having my granddaughter with me, you're a fool."

A shocked silence settled over the table. No one had expected to hear Grandma lash out like that.

Mama giggled, then held a menu in front of her face, her eyes laughing above it.

Mr. Clayton turned his hands palms up. "Of course you have. Of course you have. But an active ten-year-old must keep you on your toes."

"Don't you worry about my toes," Grandma snapped.

At the same time, Lexie said, insulted, "I'm eleven, almost twelve!" Her thoughts whirled. This was what she'd wanted—to be with Mama. It didn't matter where. So why did she feel all mixed up? *Mama means to go, whether I go or not.*

"She doesn't have clothes with her for such a trip," Grandma said, as if that settled the matter and Lexie wouldn't be going.

The suitcase Lexie had packed so full leaped into her mind. She had come prepared to stay with Mama. But somehow the first rush of excitement was fading.

In her breezy way, Mama said, "When we get to Japan, we'll find a seamstress to sew you some glad rags, kiddo. Maybe a kimono! You'll be cute as a button!"

"You need to think about this, Electra," Grandma warned, the pain easy to see on her face.

Lexie felt hot and cold by turns. She had aimed her whole life — well, the past several months — toward getting back to Mama. But she wished the surprise had been a kitten after all.

It wasn't a kitten. And she had to make a decision that felt too big for her. "I've already thought about it."

"Swell!" Mama exclaimed. "You and me in Japan, kiddo. We're going to be the bee's knees!"

"No," Lexie said, feeling bad about disappointing Mama. But her decision felt more and more like the right one. She wondered if that decision had been growing since she'd learned it wasn't Toby who had kept Mama from meeting the ship, even though she hadn't known about the trip and the decision until just now.

Everyone was looking at her. She had to tell them all. "I'm going to Portland with Grandma." Tears threatened, and she swallowed hard. "When you come back, you can stay with us for a while. Can't she, Grandma?"

"Of course." Grandma looked like someone who had won a big prize and was trying not to cheer in front of the losers. "You're always welcome, Thea."

"But sweetie," Mama protested, "this chance won't come again. Take time to think about it. You have to be sure."

Lexie thought of the way Captain Richards had looked at Mama, a look Lexie had seen before. That look meant dancing all night while Lexie waited alone in a cabin.

Japan would be exciting while Mama was with her, full of energy and excitement and laughter. But Lexie knew she'd be spending a lot of time alone in Japan, where people talked in a language she didn't know and wouldn't understand. She had spent a lot of time alone in Seattle but hadn't let herself think about that. She had to think about it now. "I am sure."

"Why?" Grandma sounded as if she didn't want to risk changing Lexie's mind but felt she had to give her that chance.

Lexie looked from one to the other around the table. She searched for a reason to turn down the trip that wouldn't hurt Mama. And found one. "Grandpa says Japan might go to war with China. He said we might get into it, too."

"If we see a hint of war coming," Mr. Clayton assured her, "we'll skedaddle home."

"There won't be a war," Mama said. "When

did you become such a worrier? We could have a hoot over there!" Beneath the sparkle in her eyes, sadness glimmered.

"It's more than maybe a war," Lexie said, trying to explain. "I need to be here. I need to be with Grandma and Grandpa and Jack and my friends at school and . . . and come summer, I have a cherry pit–spitting contest to win."

Grandma sucked in a startled breath, but Mama nodded. "That's my kid!" Quietly she added, "You know I love you?"

"Yes," She did know that. She had never doubted Mama's love. And never would. "I love you, too. I'll be waiting when you come back."

In the morning Lexie stood with Grandma, watching Mama wave from the big ship's rail. Mama had glowed the way she always did when she hugged good-bye, but some of the shine in her eyes came from tears.

"You'll be back," Lexie told her, holding tightly and wondering how to let go or if she could.

"Of course I'll be back!" Mama kissed the top of her head, then gently held her away to look at her, as if memorizing her face. "Next time, kiddo, you and me, we'll go together."

Then, while Lexie clung to Grandma's hand, fighting the urge to break away, to run after Mama and drag her from the ship, her mama walked up the gangplank. She turned with almost every step to wave again.

When the gangplank was drawn in and the anchor pulled up and all the chains released, two tugboats nudged the big ship away from the dock. Lexie jumped up and down beside Grandma, waving until she couldn't make out Mama among the other people crowding the rail.

The tugs guided the ship up the bay. All too soon, it was lost to sight among others lining the piers. She didn't have to see it to picture the tugs returning while the ship churned through the channel into the Pacific Ocean to begin the journey to Japan.

She swallowed hard, wondering if it was all right to cry now that Mama couldn't see her. But she had held the tears back for so long, they felt locked inside.

"You made the right choice," Grandma said. "And I'm as thankful as it's possible to be that I'm not watching you sailing away to a foreign country." She hesitated. "But, honey, I'm sorry your grandpa scared you with all his grumblings. Like as not, your mama's right. There won't be any war."

"I had another reason." Lexie put her hand on Grandma's comfortable, familiar arm. "It's that . . . you would have met my ship that day, no matter who else wanted you with them."

"You know I would." Grandma caught her into a tighter hug than any she'd given Lexie before. When she let her go, her eyes looked shiny, and she said again softly, "You know I would."

Lexie felt right with Grandma holding her. They'd had some awful arguments not so long ago, and she knew they might have more ahead. But she was glad to be here on the dock with Grandma. The tears came loose after all and streaked down her face. Blinking, she looked toward the ship, although she could no longer see it. "Will she be safe?"

"Your mama always finds her way. She'll come back before you know it."

Lexie hoped Grandma was right. It was hard not to think about Grandpa's predictions when he read the paper or listened to news on the radio. If Mama and the dolls were sailing into a country about to start a war, she hoped Mama would give up her adventure and sail straight back across the ocean.

But Mama had to make her own choices. Lexie had made hers. She looked at Grandma and smiled, the mist gone from her eyes. "Let's go home and see if Louise tells the truth at school."

AUTHOR'S NOTE

Lexie's story is fiction based on a little-known event in American-Japanese history, the exchange of Friendship Dolls between children of both countries. The dolls were meant to help American and Japanese children understand and love one another so they would grow up to wish for peace with their friends across the Pacific.

The project was begun by Dr. Sidney Gulick, who retired to America after years of teaching in Japan. In 1924, out of fear of losing American jobs to immigrants, American lawmakers passed an act barring new Japanese immigration to the United

States — a law that was not rescinded until 1954. Sensing the danger of a coming war, Dr. Gulick urged American children to join his project.

In nearly every one of the then forty-eight American states, children collected pennies to buy, dress, and transport dolls for Japan. Records usually give the number of dolls sent as 12,739. (A listing of dolls received by each Japanese prefecture totals 12,294.) Whatever the correct total may be, more than twelve thousand dolls made the journey.

They traveled by steamship to Yokohama, arriving in time for the annual Girls' Day festival called Hinamatsuri, which features ceremonial dolls kept by families.

The American dolls were welcomed with parades and parties. Several young Japanese princesses attended the biggest celebration of all. A Japanese newspaper wrote, "The exchange of dolls is the exchange of hearts."

In response, the Japanese government commissioned its finest doll makers to create fifty-eight elegant Japanese dolls, each thirty-three inches tall, to travel to America. These dolls represented each of the forty-seven prefectures, the four territories, and the six major cities of Japan. The fifty-eighth, an especially elegant and expensive doll named Miss Dai Nippon (Miss Japan), was given by the imperial household.

As with the American dolls, each carried a letter from a Japanese child, along with traveling clothes, a steamship ticket, and a passport. Unlike the American dolls, these traveled in first-class cabins. Each doll came with accessories to illustrate Japanese life, including tea sets for daily and ceremonial use, lacquered chests and tiered tables, silk-shaded lamps, and even tiny toys and dolls of their own. The dolls' faces were made of a composite using crushed oyster shell. They were dressed in elegant kimonos made of handprinted or delicately painted silk.

Called the Dolls of Gratitude, the Japanese dolls arrived in America in November 1927, in time for Christmas. Some toured America while others waited in New York City. The dolls were warmly welcomed with parties and celebrations, then displayed in museums throughout America.

Sadly, the Friendship Dolls could not prevent war between the two countries. In 1941, after Japanese planes bombed American navy ships at Pearl Harbor, America joined World War II.

What of the dolls? In America, the lovely kimonoed Miss Japan and her sisters were stored away and forgotten. The dolls in Japan suffered a harder fate. In 1943, they were declared "symbols of the enemy." The government ordered them destroyed, often in front of the children who had come to love them.

However, friendship had already blossomed between American and Japanese girls, many of whom exchanged letters before the war. Adults by the time the dolls were ordered destroyed, a few brave young women secretly defied their government by hiding dolls throughout those devastating years.

World War II ended in 1945. Reconstruction began in Japan. Cities rose. Trade flourished, and the two countries became friends.

Beginning around 1973, the remaining American Friendship Dolls (often called the Blue-Eyed Dolls) were remembered and gradually recovered from their hiding places. Nearly three hundred were eventually rescued and placed on display.

In America, the Japanese Dolls of Gratitude were also rediscovered and rescued from storage areas and dusty basements. At this writing, forty-six of the original fifty-eight dolls have been restored and placed on display in museums across the country.

More information, along with both historic and contemporary photographs, can be found at http://www.bill-gordon.net/dolls/.